THE FOURTH PIG

ODDLY MODERN FAIRY TALES
JACK ZIPES, SERIES EDITOR

Oddly Modern Fairy Tales is a series dedicated to publishing unusual literary fairy tales produced mainly during the first half of the twentieth century. International in scope, the series includes new translations, surprising and unexpected tales by well-known writers and artists, and uncanny stories by gifted yet neglected authors. Postmodern before their time, the tales in *Oddly Modern Fairy Tales* transformed the genre and still strike a chord.

Naomi Mitchison, *The Fourth Pig*

Kurt Schwitters, *Lucky Hans and Other Merz Fairy Tales*

Béla Balázs, *The Cloak of Dreams: Chinese Fairy Tales*

Peter Davies, editor, *The Fairies Return: Or, New Tales for Old*

THE
FOURTH
PIG

NAOMI MITCHISON

WITH A NEW INTRODUCTION BY
MARINA WARNER

Princeton University Press
Princeton and Oxford

Published by arrangement with Kennedy & Boyd
(www.kennedyandboyd.co.uk)
Requests for permission to reproduce material from this work
should be sent to Permissions, Princeton University Press
Published by Princeton University Press, 41 William Street,
Princeton, New Jersey 08540
In the United Kingdom: Princeton University Press, 6 Oxford Street,
Woodstock, Oxfordshire OX20 1TW
First published in 1936 by Constable and Company Ltd., London,
and the Macmillan Company of Canada, Ltd., Toronto

press.princeton.edu

The frontispiece and title page were designed by Gertrude Hermes
Jacket Art: Bunches of hay © An Nguyen; piles of firewood © GoodMood
Photo; brick wall © antpkr. All images courtesy Shutterstock.
Jacket design by Jessica Massabrook.

ISBN 978–0-691–15895–2
Library of Congress Control Number 2013954729

British Library Cataloging-in-Publication Data is available

This book has been composed in Cronos Pro & Adobe Jenson Pro

Printed on acid-free paper. ∞

Printed in the United States of America

1 3 5 7 9 10 8 6 4 2

CONTENTS

INTRODUCTION

> I have said very little here about my writing. It is my job and I
> think I do it well. In some ways my writing is old-fashioned, but
> I doubt if that matters much. . . . I know I can handle words, the
> way other people handle colours or computers or horses.
> —Naomi Mitchison, aged 90[1]

Reviewing a book by the poet Stevie Smith in 1937, the year after
The Fourth Pig was published, Naomi Mitchison opened with a
characteristic *cri de coeur*: "Because I myself care passionately
about politics, because I am part of that 'we' which I am willing to
break my heart over, and can no longer properly feel myself an 'I,'
because that seems to me to be the right thing for me to do and
be, I see no reason why everyone has got to. Stevie Smith can still
be an 'I.' And that's good." She is thinking about her contemporary's enviable singularity of experience and voice: "Such people
don't have to be 'we'; they can be 'I,' proudly and bouncingly as

I would like to thank Graeme Mitchison and Sally Mitchison very much indeed for shar-
ing thoughts about their grandmother, and for commenting most helpfully on the draft of
this essay. My profound thanks also to Gill Plain, Ali Smith, Graeme Segal, and Kate
Arnold-Foster for their help with readings and responses, and to the editor of this series,
the indefatigable and inspired Jack Zipes.
1   Naomi Mitchison, *Saltire Self-Portraits 2* (Edinburgh: The Saltire Society, 1986), p.
32; see also Elizabeth Maslen, "Mitchison, Naomi Mary Margaret, Lady Mitchison
(1897–1999)," *Oxford Dictionary of National Biography* (Oxford University Press, 2004;
online ed., May 2009, http://www.oxforddnb.com/view/article/50052, accessed 30
Aug. 2009); Diana Wallace, "Naomi Mitchison," *The Literary Encyclopedia*, 14 Nov. 2005.

Blake was. . . . Stevie Smith bounces with Blake."[2] The passage is revealing in many ways: Naomi Mitchison's style is colloquial, vigorous, and unsentimental; it drew praise from E. M. Forster, for example, for the directness with which she brought distant, exotic characters to life before the reader's eyes. Furthermore, the review reveals her generosity of spirit: where some critics might inflict a wound, she embraces a potential rival or adversary, insisting on others' democratic right to difference. But above all, her sense that she belonged to a group or a class, rather than enjoyed the free play of subjectivity like the visionary Blake, or the inspired eccentric Stevie Smith, reflects an anguished split deep down in Naomi Mitchison's consciousness.

She was right to recognise this division in herself, between public duty and private vision, between communal feeling and personal passion, between elite learning and popular lore. She was torn all her life between her intellectual, feminist ambitions and her wealthy, patrician upbringing and way of life—"the incalculable advantages" of her background, as Vera Brittain put it.[3] "Nou" Mitchison, née Haldane, was a woman from "the Big House," as she put it in the title of a story for children.

Her double consciousness created further tensions that pull her writing this way and that, between solemnity and frivolity, mandarin and demotic language, between playful ingenuousness and harsh defiance of convention. She was born in 1897; her

2 Quoted in Frances Spalding, *Stevie Smith: A Critical Biography* (London: Faber & Faber, 1988), p. 131.

3 Vera Brittain, *Testament of Youth* (London: Victor Gollancz, 1993), quoted in Ali Smith, "The Woman from the Big House: The Autobiographical Writings of Naomi Mitchison," (1987) introduction to Naomi Mitchison, *Small Talk . . . Memories of an Edwardian Childhood* (1973) (Glasgow: Kennedy & Boyd (2009), p. vii.

mother and father were divided in their political—and social—opinions and attendant social mores. Her Tory mother was horrified, for instance, when Naomi made friends "behind the counter at the small draper's in North Parade": as a result Naomi was "severely lectured about trade."[4] Naomi's girlhood was enmeshed in dynastic kinship systems; her grandparents were wealthy landowners in Scotland, with huge, chilly castles, salmon brooks, deer-stalking, while her parents, by contrast, were Liberal and progressive and brilliant. Her father, John S. Haldane, was a distinguished medical biologist at Oxford and, deeply concerned for working men and women, led pioneering work on lung disease at the beginning of the century, diagnosing the miasmas that killed in the mines, factories, and mills of industrialised Britain. He also helped invent the first gas masks for protection in World War I. His concerns shaped his two children more profoundly than his wife's sense of class and etiquette.

Naomi's older brother, J.B.S. (Jack) Haldane, made an even greater mark, as a geneticist and biologist. He was a colossal personality, and his transgressiveness, independent-mindedness, and sheer cleverness set a bar for Naomi she was always longing to leap. He was a free, even wayward spirit—sacked from Cambridge for adultery with a colleague's wife (he married her), he became a Communist, and later, an Indian nationalist, renouncing his British citizenship. When they were children, they'd been allies and equals and sparring partners; they played charades and dressed up, putting on plays they wrote themselves; they experimented together on scientific questions, cross-breeding coloured

4 Mitchison, *Small Talk*, p. 50.

guinea pigs, and cutting up a caterpillar—this last was intended to be a rug for the dolls' house, but it shrivelled (a lesson in life and death).

After this enchanted though stormy alliance, Jack was sent away to school (Eton), whereas Naomi had to stay at home. Before then she had been a rare girl attending the boys' Dragon School in Oxford. Jack's going away, the arrival of a governess for all-important lessons in decorum, the new ban on climbing trees, all gave Naomi a bitter taste of gender injustices. The title of *Small Talk* (1973), a marvelous, witty, and tender memoir about her childhood, catches the stifling restrictions she suffered, and she never overcame her ferocious jealousy of her brother. Consequently Jack dominates his little sister's fiction in various little-disguised heroic personae. But her imagination also stamped out in her stories one spirited daredevil young woman after another—wild girls, strong-limbed and tousled, who break rules, act vigorously, and reject mincing and simpering. This is what I found in her books when I was young, when I too was furious that being female still prevented me from being as free as a male.

Naomi, the faery child, had intense dreams and kept open the connection to childlike wonder and terror. "I met a brown hare," she remembers, "and we went off and kept house (marriage as I saw it) inside a corn stook with six oat sheaves propped around us." She did not know then, she continued, that the hare is closely associated with the moon and the goddess, as well as with witchcraft. "As I remember it, I was married young to the hare."[5]

5   Ibid., p. 33.

The bride of the hare was also a bookworm and a hungry listener, especially to the many charismatic friends and lovers in her long life. By the time she was sixteen, she had read all the way through the complete *Golden Bough* of J. G. Frazer: relations between magic and society, and regeneration rituals involving dying kings and tree cults, run a live current of atavistic ecstasy through her work. The Greek myths and Celtic—especially Scottish—lore, predominate, chiefly because she was brought up among Oxford classicists and spent her summers in the Highlands, on the Cloan estate of her "Granniema," until she moved to her own home, Carradale, in Argyll in 1937. These two potent, intertwined influences from north and south were also often under tension: on the one hand she was drawn to neo-paganism, which was founded in scholarship and a broad curiosity about European magical wisdom; and on the other she was wrapped in the Celtic Twilight, which focused on the Scottish legends and folklore of her forebears and, later, of her chosen home in Argyll. In the Edwardian period, these varieties of supernatural experience burgeoned into correspondingly contrasting uses of enchantment: first, avant-garde demands for liberty (Nietzsche's vision flows in Jane Harrison's Greek scholarship and infuses *The Rite of Spring*; the D. H. Lawrence of *The Plumed Serpent* turns to myth for reinvigoration of the life principle), and second, traditionalist nostalgia for a lost, enchanted pastoral, reflected in some of the most celebrated fantasy classics, such as *Peter Pan*, by a fellow Scot, J. M. Barrie; Kenneth Grahame's *Wind in the Willows* (1908); and A. A. Milne's stories of Winnie the Pooh (who makes his first appearance in 1926).

After Naomi Mitchison moved to Scotland, she became some-thing of a Scottish nationalist, but before that she was already striving, as evident in this collection, to combine the Gaelic tradi-tions of fairyland with myths of gods and goddesses. She also adopted traditional oral forms, such as tales and ballads, histori-cal epic, praise song, flyting, charms, and elegy. As the stories in this book show, she relished tales of changelings, fairy abduc-tions, and the local population of bogles, boggarts, and other el-dritch folk in the Highlands. Walking past a deserted village on her way home one evening, she ran into the "botoch" or spirit of a villager who haunted the place. He had been eaten alive by rats. She was only able to pass after she had recited a Gaelic charm she knew—or so she related to one of her grandsons. The past, both as recoverable imaginable history and as a granary of story, served to open ways of picturing possibilities for the present. She culti-vated her imagination with the deliberateness of an experimental scientist, in order to move on, into a dreamed-of, better future.

In 1916, when she was not yet twenty, she married Dick Mitch-ison, who was a friend of her brother Jack's; he was also very young (b. 1894), a soldier in the Queen's Bays infantry regiment and about to fight in France; he was badly wounded in the head almost immediately in a motorbike accident as he was carrying dispatches; but he returned to the trenches, rose to become a Major, and was awarded the Croix de Guerre. In civil life he be-came a lawyer, and a distinguished Queen's Counsel; together they grew to share overwhelming indignation at the social condi-tions in England. He entered parliament as a Labour MP amid the bright hopes of the 1945 Attlee government, and was later ennobled (though Naomi did not use the title "Lady Mitchison").

Their marriage was long, turbulent but strong, both of them accepting each other's lovers as friends. After the shock she felt during her first experiences of sex as a very young wife, which she wrote about frankly and bravely, Naomi struck out for freedoms (such as contraception, abortion, and open marriage) with more courage than many in her social circle. Nevertheless, she had six children, losing her firstborn, a boy, to meningitis at the age of 9, and a daughter shortly after birth, events which surface in anguish in many of her books.

Naomi Mitchison conjures up ardent tomboy heroines in homage to the dream of freedom she had entertained before the conventions of class and gender put her in shackles. She imagines them as paragons of desire and autonomy in faraway settings—in ancient Egypt, Scythia, Sparta, Gaul, Constantinople, Rome, Scotland, or Hell, where they can act as daughters of her longings, and she wanted them to beckon to her readers as irresistibly as any fairy from the fairy hill. Several stories in this collection, such as "Soria Moria Castle" and "Adventure in the Debateable Land," and Kate Crackernuts herself, present such figures of female liberators.

She also wanted to prove that science—her father and Jack's preserve in her family—could be reconciled with fantasy, which was her own strength. She refused to allow the latter to be dismissed by the former. In an attempt to rekindle magic in modern, rational times, she plays with wilful anachronisms. The technique is a form of defamiliarisation: she takes the humdrum and queers it. Slang falls from the lips of the gods ("What utter bilge, Xanthias," says Dionysos in "Frogs and Panthers"). Later in the same story, the god returns in a motorcar, smoking. In this updated classical myth, Mitchison kneads together her lingering conscience about belonging to the upper class, her solidarity with the workers, and her memories of her father's work on the respiratory horrors of industrial towns in the north. She wanted to refresh tradition, and feared what she called "the archaistic view."

The literary scholar Gill Plain recently commented that Mitchison "creatively politicised history, using it as a space through which to imagine 'an abstract future postwar,' and to challenge the assumptions of patriarchal history."[6] She reaches backwards in time, and reconstructs a better, more intense, more conscious, more meaningful experience in the past for several periods and peoples and cultures. History, retooled, is then shot through with magic and mythic effects. The Debateable Land that is the literary terrain of myth and fairy tale set her free to imagine what she longed for—or sometimes feared.

Naomi Mitchison was one of the splendid unstoppable graphomaniacs of her day, to put alongside prodigal precursors and authors of her youth (Mrs Oliphant, Walter Scott, H. G. Wells); she published nearly a hundred books, as well as hundreds of articles, reviews, and blasts in the papers, not to mention her private letters (she and her husband, when apart, would correspond on a daily basis until the Thirties). Writing became as necessary to her existence as breathing or eating: a form of health-giving exercise. She was of the generation of women who went in for emancipatory athletics, as in the Women's League of Health and Beauty. Her activity was writing. There is hardly a genre she did

---

6 Gill Plain, *Women's Fiction of the Second World War: Gender, Power and Resistance* (Edinburgh: Edinburgh University Press, 1996), p. 154.

not attempt, a reader whose interests she did not try to capture, or a world of experience she did not enter.

The struggle between the good citizen and the wild girl, the nurse and the sorceress, runs through the whole of her astounding body of work. It accounts, too, for the neglect that she has fallen into for some time now. For it is a bit of mystery that this once best-selling novelist, polemicist, memoirist, and *grande dame* of letters, who came from a fabulous intellectual lineage, was englamoured by wealth and prestige (at least for part of her lifetime), and led an intrepid experimental life in her work and her loves, should not have captured more attention since her death in 1999 at the age of 101. After all, the Haldanes were formidable scientists, eccentric, spirited, politically activist, and far richer than, for example, the Mitfords, who have inspired shelf-loads of admiration. Naomi wrote several times, with wry, comic vividness, about her family's charmed life before the Second World War, with many forbidding aunts and grandparents, crowded households of servants to meet every need, and much nonchalant possession of dark labyrinthine mansions; her memoirs give off a wonderful whiff of Blandings Castle and the immortal Aunt Agatha of Wodehouse's imagination. The novelist Ali Smith has commented warmly on "the overall frank friendliness" of her voice in these books.[7] Naomi Mitchison seems ripe for Bloomsbury-style fandom.

But she does not command this kind of following, and the problems that her writing poses for contemporary readers stem from that split she rightly diagnosed between the "we" and the "I"

7   Smith, "Woman from the Big House," p. vii.

in her makeup. Some of the writers with whom she could be compared—contemporaries such as Virginia Woolf (b. 1882) and Elizabeth Bowen (b. 1899), and others who were close friends, Wyndham Lewis (b. 1882) and Aldous Huxley (b. 1894)—were naturally modern. Whether by instinct, default, or choice, such writers belonged to the twentieth century and conveyed features of the time without needing to check their watches. But Naomi Mitchison is only partly modern. Or perhaps, as in the title which Jack Zipes has given this series, she was oddly, but not entirely, modern. This quality, her faltering modernity, arises from many features of her life and work.[8]

Chiefly, she felt deep loyalty to a whole array of groups, with whom she cultivated a sense of belonging, and for whom she spoke. They were the "we" who shadowed her throughout her life: they changed identity, but, at one period or another, Soviet workers, oppressed women and mothers, sharecroppers in the South of the United States, Scottish crofters and fishermen, Botswana nationalists, all claimed her attention.

The love of enchantment flourished alongside practical activity: farming, campaigning for Scottish development and for the community around her—a lively fictionalized memoir, *Lobsters on the Agenda* (1952), chronicles her efforts on behalf of local fisheries. She was also actively involved in the independence of Botswana, where she became a tribal elder. Jenni Calder gave her 1997 biography the title *The Nine Lives of Naomi Mitchison*, but nine is an understatement. Mitchison unleashed her forces in all

---

8 The terms "intermodern" and "intermodernist" have been suggested in relation to Mitchison and contemporaries; see Further Reading for critical studies by Hubble, Lassner, Montefiore, Maslen (see note 1), and Mackay and Stonebridge.

these areas, as well as giving voice to her unstoppable imaginative powers, in book after book, article after article. Among nearly a hundred publications, the heroes and heroines she brings to life before us often represent a cause. To an exceptional degree, Mitchison's torrential energies were directed at making a difference to others, and there is sometimes too much of a sense that she has designs on her text, and on you, her reader.

Naomi Mitchison's less than complete modernity also stems from her passionate belief in the mythical imagination. She fought to defend it against the high status of rationality and scepticism, advocated by family and friends. She also liked witches and witchcraft, and in her ferocious magnum opus, *The Corn King and the Spring Queen* (1931), she creates a towering, complex self-portrait in the character of Erif Der (Red Fire backwards), who has the gift of spellbinding, and uses it to powerful but often troubling effect. She felt animosity towards D. H. Lawrence, on account of his view of dominant male sexuality, but she shares some of his love of primitivism and ritual. In spite of her distaste for archaism, archaism colours her passionate imagination, adding a streak of neo-paganism that has been relegated from current versions of modernity. It can make her a bit old-fashioned, as she herself recognised in later years.

Mitchison the writer saw herself as an enchantress, and she liked to attract a large company around her, of children, family, friends, and retainers. In the Fifties, at her home in Carradale on the beautiful Mull of Kintyre in Scotland, a family friend called Charlie Brett painted the doors of a cupboard with a romantic panorama of the house standing in the magnificent landscape. Naomi figures there as Circe, standing on the threshold facing the sea, where Dionysos' vine-wreathed barque is sailing by and Ulysses is approaching in his boat, while local fisher folk, friends, guests, shepherds, villagers are also transmuted into creatures from myth and fairy tale. Scotland was Attica, or Thrace, or Calypso's Isle—or Circe's.

Several of the friends in the circle of her passionate attachments can be glimpsed in the wings of these fairy tales: "Granddaughter" is written for Stella Benson, a kindred spirit, feminist and writer, who had died of pneumonia in 1933. G.D.H.C., the dedicatee of "Soria Moria Castle," is Douglas Cole, who was the husband of Margaret Cole; she was a longtime lover of Naomi's husband, Dick. In "Birmingham and the Allies," which describes the Labour defeat in 1931 and Dick's initial failure to win a seat in parliament, his election team are included by name, including his agent, Tom Baxter. The dedication of "Mirk, Mirk Night"—"for strange roads, with Zita"—alludes to Naomi's travels in Alabama with the adventurous activist Zita Baker, when the two women joined the sharecroppers in their fight for better conditions, outraged the local white inhabitants, and had a great deal of fun. Her obituary in the *Guardian* rightly commented, "There was a Fabian, Shavian flavour to her energy; she could have belonged to the 'Fellowship for a new Life.'"[9]

The commitment to fantasy takes a lyric songlike form, as in some of the writings in this collection, and also often tends to comedy (sometimes inadvertently—the "Chinese fairies" in "Birmingham and the Allies" don't quite bring the comrades to mind as they should). Sometimes this British taste for feyness and

9   Neal Ascherson, "Naomi Mitchison—a Queen, a Saint and a Shaman," *Guardian*, 17 Jan. 1999.

nonsense has the effect of undermining the strength of her dreams. Her rational side refused to allow full surrender to the seductions of fairyland—she is clear that she doesn't believe in the supernatural, but her fictions are driven by its forces and structured by ritual. At her best, Naomi Mitchison is forthright and witty, writes with brio and passion and lucidity, and conveys a huge appetite for life, for people, for new adventures, and for breaking through barriers. At her worst, she damages her serious purposes with whimsy, sometimes with wishful thinking, and sometimes with lurid bacchanalian violence. Her writing is a bit hit-and-miss, but her personality is colossal and wonderful.

Towards the end of her life, Mitchison was disappointed by the neglect of her work: she was no longer Circe or the oracle at Delphi or Cumae, but Cassandra, and was not being heard. The political ideals for which she and her family had battled were being mothballed; she was born under Queen Victoria when Gladstone was Prime Minister and died under Tony Blair and New Labour: the span reveals a changed world, and the dashing of progressive hopes and dreams.

The tales in *The Fourth Pig* are a "misch-masch," as Lewis Carroll called his first such compilation, the album of miscellanea he made up to amuse his siblings. Naomi Mitchison customarily wove prose and poetry together in her fiction, and published such anthologies throughout her career, refusing to rank genres of storytelling, or to make a hierarchy of different belief systems or manifestations of the supernatural. Fairy tales were not inferior to myth or myths lesser than religion. Some of the stories she reworks here are very well known ("Hansel and Gretel"; "The

Little Mermaiden"); in others she picks up the tune of a ballad with admiring fidelity to the form ("Mairi Maclean and the Fairy Man"); several of the tales involve experimental twists of her own. The reverie of Brünnhilde as she floats down the Rhine takes its place beside a fairy play *Kate Crackernuts*, dramatising in charms and songs a struggle against the subterranean powers who live in the fairy hills of Scotland and abduct humans for their pleasure.

The story of Kate Crackernuts was collected by Andrew Lang in the Orkneys and included by the folklorist Joseph Jacobs in *English Fairy Tales* (1890; a misnomer, but an inspired and foundational anthology). Naomi Mitchison adapted it as a lively fairy-tale play in verse, written, as the stage directions show, for family theatricals. The story inverts the fairy tale "The Twelve Dancing Princesses," as it features a spellbound prince instead, who is stolen away to dance all night in fairyland. The play version here also carries strong echoes of Christina Rossetti's famous poem "Goblin Market," which similarly stages an epic struggle between two loving sisters and the rescue of one by the other. In Mitchison's version, Ann is transmogrified by Kate's cruel mother, and given a horrible sheep's head, while Kate's rescue mission introduces a heterosexual love plot, not found in Rossetti. The play also recalls the terrible wound and subsequent delirium and illness that Dick Mitchison, Naomi's young husband, suffered in World War I, and her long vigil at his bedside as he pulled through. It is characteristic of Naomi Mitchison's spirit that she dramatises a girl's heroic knight errantry on his behalf. The same memories haunt the poignant closing story in the collection, "Mirk, Mirk Night," but the heroine here is herself rescued from the fairies by the hero, who "smelt of tobacco and machine oil and his own smell," suffers from the shivers from shell shock, and yet delivers her from the beguiling, shining, and crying of the trooping fairies in pursuit.

The belief in the danger posed by fairies from the fairy hills was recorded by the Reverend Robert Kirk in the manuscript of his parishioners' beliefs, drawn up at the end of the seventeenth century. Walter Scott, who reinvigorated the folk and fairy lore of Scotland, was the first to write about Kirk's astonishing anthology, but it was not published until 1893, when Andrew Lang edited it under the new title *The Secret Commonwealth of Elves, Fauns and Fairies*, and supported its accounts of Second Sight and other paranormal and curious powers.[10] Andrew Lang was a family friend of the Mitchisons, and Lang's appetite for legends, history, and fantasy can also be strongly felt in Naomi's combination of proud localism and voracious eclecticism. Beginning with *The Blue Fairy Book* in 1889, he edited stories from all over the world in anthologies for children that were revised and generally standardised and cleaned up by his wife, Leonora Alleyne, and other female scribes. In spite of this bland tendency, Lang's collections were wildly successful, and have influenced generations of writers, including the preeminent English fabulist Angela Carter (1941–1992), whose fierce, baroque revisionings of classic fairy tales in her collection *The Bloody Chamber* (1979) took the erotic supernatural to a pitch of intensity that Naomi Mitchison would have relished.

---

10   Robert Kirk, *The Secret Commonwealth of Elves, Fauns and Fairies*, ed. Andrew Lang, with introduction by Marina Warner (New York: *New York Review of Books*, 2007).

Later in life Naomi declared that she "never much cared for the more romantic series of fairy tales in spite of their lovely pictures."[11] The "lovely pictures," mostly by H. J. Ford, depict details of jewels and clothing with a heightened, Pre-Raphaelite realism that chimes with Mitchison's love of vivid description. Like Carter and unlike Lang, Mitchison avoided the *Fairy Books'* rather solemn politeness; by contrast she relished transgression and a certain degree of delinquent extremism—especially in her female characters. Her stories are filled with daring steps across the threshold of permitted normative behaviour, and often open into scenes of extraordinary erotic, savage violence, as in the fertility rituals dramatized in *The Corn King and the Spring Queen*. Here, in *Kate Crackernuts*, similar reverberations from Frazerian fertility ritual break through:

Fairy:
Shall we take her, shall we keep her?
In the harvest of the foe
Shall we bind, shall we reap her?
In the Green Hill deeper
Shall we stack her, hold her, keep her?

Sick Prince (with hate):
Take her, take her,
Bind her, blind her! (Act II, scene III)

Around this time Mitchison was close to Wyndham Lewis, and he illustrated an exuberant, crazy, phantasmagoric quest

11   Ibid., p. 51.

story she wrote in 1935, *Beyond This Limit*, about an artist called Phoebe, who, armed with an alarmingly live crocodile handbag, cures herself of a broken heart and sets out for freedom.[12] It begins in a *salon de thé* in a recognisable present-day Paris, but turns into a fugue through surrealist dreamlands populated by creatures out of the *Alice* books or one of Leonora Carrington's comic fables. But Mitchison is aware that not all her heroines succeed in cutting the traces of convention. The "Snow Maiden" in this collection is a promising mathematician, but boys and peer pressure and social expectations drive the brains out of a girl: "So Mary Snow got married to George Higginson, and then—well then, she just seemed to melt away . . . like an ice-cream sundae on a hot afternoon. . . . Some girls do seem to go like that after they get married." Jenni Calder comments that this bleak satire targets Lawrence.

The story which gives the collection its title, *The Fourth Pig*, foresees the impending horror of World War II with a clarity very few possessed in the Thirties: the jolly nursery classic of three little pigs has taken a dark turn, and their youngest sibling knows the nature of the Wolf: "I can smell the Wolf's breath above all the sweet smells of Spring and the rich smells of Autumn. I can hear the padding of the Wolf's feet a very long way off in the forest, coming nearer. And I know there is no way of stopping him. Even if I could help being afraid. But I cannot help it. I am afraid now."

Her brother Jack openly adopted Marxism in 1937, and Naomi herself was forthright in her support for the Republican side in

12　NM, *Beyond This Limit: Selected Shorter Fiction of Naomi Mitchison*, ed. Isobel Murray (Edinburgh: Association of Scottish Literary Studies, 1986), pp. 1–83.

the Spanish Civil War, which was raging as she was putting together *The Fourth Pig*: "There is no question for any decent, kindly man or woman," she wrote, "let alone a poet or writer who must be more sensitive. We have to be against Franco and Fascism and for the people of Spain, and the future of gentleness and brotherhood which ordinary men and women want all over the world."[13] The "black bulls of hate" in "Pause in the Corrida" evoke the conflict directly, but much of the collection's feeling of dread and darkness seeps through its pages from the implications of the Fascists gaining ground elsewhere as well.

In 1935 Mitchison had published *We Have Been Warned*, the only novel she set in her own time and place; it was unflinchingly honest—dismayingly so, to her contemporaries. Although the eventual publishers (Constable; others refused the risk) censored her original version, she was still too frank about sex for the critics: she sets down with her usual vigour the sexual difficulties and disappointments that she knew from experience, gives a picture of free love without apology, and describes her lovers using contraceptives—conveyed with a feminist practicality which eluded Lawrence, for example. But Naomi was not yet used to criticism, as her earlier fictions, from *The Conquered* (1923) onwards, had all been enthusiastically received—and widely read.

In the story here called "Grand-daughter," a child looks back, from some unidentified point in the future, at the times of her grandmother's generation, and wonders at their blindness. The little girl expresses her surprise at the foolishness of her elders in those distant days, the 1930s. She is imagined, by Naomi, leafing

13   John Simkin, *Spanish Civil War* (Spartacus Educational, 2012, http://www.spartacus.schoolnet.co.uk/Wmitchison.htm, accessed 14 June 2013).

through books produced in the decade, books like *The Fourth Pig*, and marvelling at what their authors missed. This brief, ironic piece of proleptic memoir is a kind of premature obituary, but it does show Naomi Mitchison's self-awareness. She knows she was, like the grandmother in the story, "very much laughed at for saying that the industrial revolution had destroyed magic." But the imagined grandchild of the future goes on to defend herself: "All intelligent forward-thinking people, even in the so-called imaginative professions, insisted on the recognition of their rationality and put it constantly into their talk and writing. . . . Yet, of course, that was not the whole of life." Continuing in the voice of this child in the future, Mitchison then muses on the rise of "Nazi irrationality," which "was only successful because it gave some solid fulfilment to a definite need in human beings." She castigates herself and her generation for allowing the success of fascism in Italy, Spain, and Germany. Her generation failed because they did not provide an outlet for the emotions which fascism exploited: "The rationalists stupidly feared and hated this need [for magic] . . . and refused to satisfy it decently and creatively."

The passage is an exercise in counterfactual history, but in 1936 Mitchison does not know how long and terrible the effects of fascism will be. One of these prolonged effects—part of the long shadow cast on history by those times—concerns the cult of national folklore, myth, and ritual; they were implicated in the ugliest sides of nationalism, state power, and sexual prescription, repression, and ethnic identity politics. Naomi was writing when the act of recovering the neglected fairy lore of local, unlettered folk struck a blow on behalf of the overlooked labourer, and when pagan, Dionysiac frenzy represented a belief in the arts and in freedom of expression against the choking grip of Christianity. In a letter to the poet Laura Riding at this time she expresses her anger that the Nazis have turned myth and fairy tale to their own purposes.[14] The fate of the kind of neo-paganism that Mitchison dramatized is a complicated issue, and myth and fairy tale have taken a long time to break the tainting association with right-wing nationalism. The work of fairy-tale scholars like Maria Tatar, Donald Haase, Susan Sellers, Cristina Bacchilega, and the editor of this series, Jack Zipes, has been vital in reconnecting readers with the alternative tradition—with the utopian, or often dystopian, honest fabulism of philosophical fairy tales, from Voltaire to Kafka, Karel Čapek, Kurt Schwitters, Lucy Clifford, and Angela Carter.

In the Thirties, with the Third Reich in power and the Second World War impending, fairies were being claimed for the forests of Germany, and were changing in character; fairy tales and myths, fertility rites and tree worship were annexed for ideas that were utterly repellent, and Mitchison's witchiness and whimsy no longer matched her high purposes or the needs of the times. She has glimmers of this consequence here, and it is significant that, after *The Fourth Pig*, Naomi returned to her vast historical canvases and moved back into remote times. In 1939, she published one of her most famous novels, *The Blood of the Martyrs: How the Slaves in Rome Found Victory in Christ*. As the title suggests, early Christian persecution by Nero inspires a huge and fervent mani-

---

14 NM, Letter to Laura Riding, 1 March 1937 (http://www.ntu.ac.uk/laura_riding /scholars/119214gp.html, accessed 14 June 2013).

festo for the heroic and bloody resistance of the have-nots against the haves.

Wyndham Lewis painted Naomi's portrait while she was working on the novel: she is frowning, her chin gripped by her left hand, her focus distant and intense. It is a powerful picture of a woman writing and thinking; on her right, at her shoulder, recalling her new, ardent interest in Christian sainthood, he has included an image of Jesus on Calvary, with sketches of the other two crosses for the thieves.[15]

Later still, Mitchison turned away from history to science fiction, which is a related but different kind of fantastic storytelling. In *Memoirs of a Spacewoman* (1962), she still remembers her childhood biological experiments with Jack, and imagines hermaphroditic fluidity and intelligent sex organs; she also casts herself as the saviour of caterpillars who are being inculcated with low self-esteem through telepathic communications from beautiful butterflies. She has become an astronaut, has left the fairy hill forever and taken off into outer space.

Marina Warner

---

15   The picture is in the National Galleries of Scotland.

THE FOURTH PIG

Sometimes the Wolf is quiet. He is not molesting us. It may be that he is away ravaging in far places which we cannot picture, and do not care about, or it may be that he lies up in his den, sated for the time, with half-slumberous, blood-weighted eyes, the torn flesh hot in his belly provoking miasmic evil which will turn, as he grows cold and hungry again, into some new cunning which may, after all, not be capable of frustration by the meek. For we never know. Sometimes the Wolf is stupid and can be frightened away. We may even say to ourselves that we have killed him. But more often, although we try not to think about this, the Wolf is too much for us; he refuses to be hoodwinked by the gentle or subtle. And, in the end, it is he who has the teeth and claws, the strength and the will to evil. And thus it comes, many times, that his slavering jaws crush down through broken arteries of shrieking innocents, death to the weak lamb, the merry rabbits, the jolly pigs, death to Mother Henny-penny with her downy chicks just hatched, death to Father Cocky-locky with his noble songs to the dawn, death sooner or later to Fox the inventor and story-teller, the intelligent one who yet cannot escape always. So they die in jerking agony under the sun, and the Wolf gulps them into his belly, and his juices dissolve their once lively and sentient flesh.

Sometimes the Wolf is quiet. But now the Wolf is loose and ranging and we are aware of him. We have seen in parts of our forest this Spring, how the soft leaves and air-dancing flowers have been crushed to bleeding sap, and among their green deaths come pain signs of fur and feather, of dreadful surprise and hopeless struggle. The Wolf, the Wolf has been there.

He may be hiding behind this tree or that tree. He may be disguised as kindly sheep or helpful horse. He may not be on us yet. It is possible that we shall have a breathing space. But we do not know how to use it. We cannot prepare because the Wolf never attacks the same way twice. Or he may now, at this instant, be about to spring from behind what we thought was safe and familiar. It is terrible for us to know—and not to know.

I have a pain in my head because I am trying to think about the Wolf, and the Wolf is not there to be thought about. And if he were there I could not think—I could only run, squealing. The thought of the Wolf is more than a pig's brain can hold, more than a pig's trembling, round body can be strong against. If only I could be told from which direction the Wolf would come and in what shape. We dare not be merry any longer because we are listening for the Wolf. It is too much for us. There—yes, over there—is that my friend whom I know or is it the Wolf disguised? It seems to be my friend, but I dare not trust him to come near because he might be the Wolf. Because I am not sure that he or he or he may not be the Wolf in disguise, I approach fiercely and suspiciously. One movement that reminds me of what I believe the Wolf is like, and I have struck out, I have knocked down, I have injured or killed my friend. And ah then, can I be sure that the Wolf is not in me, that I am not myself the Wolf's finally clever and successful disguise?

My three brothers live in the brick house now, and they are all afraid, even Three who was too clever for the Wolf once. But how

can he tell to what hugeness and terror the Wolf may not have
grown now? The brick house has been reinforced with steel and
concrete, so that windows and chimneys are blocked up, and the
door itself is double-barred. They cannot see the sunlight or
smell the flowers, but Three has installed a lighting and heating
plant in the cellar. He pretends it is better like that. Yet even so,
might not Wolf have so practised his huffing and puffing that
even this may not be strong enough to stand against him?

I cannot remember how it was in the time of One, in the in-
nocence of the world before thought came and memory and
foresight, and knowledge of the Wolf. Nor do I remember the
time of Two when one's house had indeed to be of stronger stuff
than the original hay, but yet after the building of it there was
dancing and singing, Maypoles and Feast-days and the village
green at evening. But I can remember a little the time of Three
who thought he knew everything and could destroy the Wolf,
although by then it should have been apparent that this is beyond our power. Oh, he was clever, was Three! He could make
things and alter things; he laughed at the others and told them
of the inevitability of the Wolf coming, but proclaimed also that
he had a sanctuary.

And so indeed it was for a time, but now he too is afraid and
there is no more playing and dancing for the others. And I am
full grown now, I am Four, without shelter and without hope. I
can sing the song still, the brave song of the pigs, crying out we
are not afraid, we have this and that and the other, and we will die
waving the Pig banner, and perhaps after we are dead there will
be something, the shadow of the rustling of bright straw, the
shadow of the taste of crunched acorns, the silver shadow of the

way back to the old sty. Something, if only we knew what it was. The song says all that, and I can sing it. I can sing it still, in the time that is left.

It may be better not to be afraid, and it may be that One and Two were truly not afraid. In the time before knowledge, in the time of dancing, none wasted thought or life in being afraid—not until the Wolf was on them, not till his teeth broke sucking into their neck-veins and the song broke into screechings. Three was afraid, but yet he thought he had the cure for fear; he thought the time would come when no pig need fear the Wolf. But I—I know I am afraid, and afraid almost all the time, even when I am singing the song; the noise of ourselves singing it doesn't keep the fear out of the back of my head any longer. I can smell the Wolf's breath above all the sweet smells of Spring and the rich smells of Autumn. I can hear the padding of the Wolf's feet a very long way off in the forest, coming nearer. And I know there is no way of stopping him. Even if I could help being afraid. But I cannot help it. I am afraid now.

OMEN OF THE ENEMY

(On Friday July 12th 1935 a cormorant, usual disguise of the Evil One,
alighted once again on the cross of St. Paul's)

Sitting once, his webbed feet furled on the flange of the cross,
His black flappers furled on the gold, the fairy bird,
The Enemy, surveys London. It is his. And the cross either
Of Paul or Jesus, having failed, must as defeat bear him.

What do you want, Bird? Bombs on London? O.K. by us.
Bombs on Berlin, Paris, where you will, the fool Swiss dove.
We've done our best for you. Now what more? Famine?—
Whose other names yet thin the brats: bread, marg and tea fed,
     nervy.
Pestilence, then? Here's measles, dip., t.b.,
Nibbling the curve of the death-rate, rickets for a bad future.
Is this what you ask, Bird? Adequate incense? We offer our all!

Sitting twice, his cold feet tight on the bright cross,
His hard flappers erect from the gold, the fairy bird,
The Enemy, croaks at London. Is it his when the cross fails?
Must then all worship? Or who stand out, face, judge break
     ranks?
Which of us not condemning our innocents to the maw of the
     cormorant,

Which of us will insist, against beak-thrusts in guts, against
    gold?
Who of us will stand, in London, will not bow down?
For the third time the Bird hovers, the cross waits.
Break down the cross if the Bird perches there, break down
All towers, castles, spires, pylons. Break even,
Oh, break Wren's London lest the webbed feet perch there,
And we, the third time, worship.

FROGS AND PANTHERS

The God Dionysos Bacchos sauntered, flame or wave shod, the delicately tawny kid-skins dangling, a short shoulder cloak, to the level of his ungirdled slim hips. Myrtle and vine buds were the lightest garland. His lyre was of Olympian gold, which is by divine law used only for ornament and in the service of the arts and sciences, and is therefore, unlike mortal gold, not corrupting, and unlike fairy gold, not heart-breaking. He held this lightly in his left hand; his right held the plectrum, ready for inspiration. The main part of the luggage, however, was bundled up in a striped blanket and carried on the end of a pole, by his slave Xanthias, the red-head, whose barbarian legs slouched across a small and unconcerned Greek donkey, which may indeed have been itself an Immortal in a small way. Dionysos and Xanthias were in the middle of a conversation. Lord Dionysos shrugged the kid-skins with one shoulder, and half turned his head to answer.

"I don't think you'll like it at all, you tiresome boy," he said rather crossly, "but of course, if you insist—"

Xanthias shook back his red head and stretched his arms out. "Free!" he said. "Free!"

"Come, come," said Lord Dionysos, "why do you fuss so, Xanthias? You don't mind taking a beating from me now and again, do you?"

"Not me," said Xanthias, "you don't hit hard enough. But there's some I've seen—"

"Some you've seen! You just trot round seeing things. And they blame it on me. You don't mind calling me Master when there's anyone about, do you? No, I thought not. You don't mind carrying the luggage. After all, if I carried it, I'd strain myself."

"And what about me?"

"Well, you don't, do you? . . . Besides, you've got the donkey to ride."

"Rotten little weasel of a donkey!"

"Well, I don't mind riding it. *I'm* not proud. *I* don't want to walk."

"Nor do I. Not with the luggage. The luggage *and* the donkey, they go together, sir, and always did. Though why you couldn't have got a mule while you were at it . . ."

"Well, I didn't. And I let you grumble all day. And I ask your advice."

"You don't take it."

"Who would? Besides, I'm an Immortal. I don't need advice. I just ask it for company's sake."

"I like that! Don't you remember last time you went to Hades—"

"Come, come, Xanthias, need we quibble? You were just the person to deal with those low types. I almost fainted from the odour. Now, don't go grinning at me that nasty way, Xanthias, you know it's every word of it true and you know I'm a good master to you. What more do you want?"

"I don't want to go on being a slave all my days, Lord Dionysos."

"Why the deuce not? My dear Xanthias, you aren't my equal, are you?"

"I can carry burdens that you can't."

"Tut! What's that to do with it? I'm an Athenian and you're a barbarian."

"I've heard you'd been seen in my parts at one time, Lord Dionysos."

"Nonsense, Xanthias! Besides, if by any chance I *did* visit you, that was for fun, not because I belonged there. No, no, my dear boy you're what Aristotle—jolly old Aristotle my dear old priceless pal—wonder what's come to him?—took up with Alexander, another of you barbarians ; ah well, one can't always keep track ... what was I saying, Xanthias? Ah yes, Aristotle called people like you natural slaves."

"If you're going in for quotations, Lord Dionysos, there was someone before Aristotle who said slavery takes away half a man's manhood. That's the way I feel."

"What utter bilge, Xanthias. Taking away your manhood indeed! Don't you remember those girls at Lady Persephone's? You accounted for twice as many as I did."

"It's not that. And you know it. But you've shown me a way out. And I'm going to take it. I won't belong ever any more to you nor to any man—"

"Oh! *God*, please."

"And I won't live my life so that anyone's got the right to take it up and twist it or throw it away! I won't have people looking at me as if I was dirt!"

"Well, Xanthias, it's in your own hands. Now, put down that bundle (which is certainly too heavy for the donkey, if not for you) and listen to me. You see that river full of frogs just in front of us. That's Anti-Styx. Instead of making you forget backwards it makes you remember forwards, and if you want to go into the time of the world when there's no more slavery, well, you can."

"You wouldn't think twice about it if you were me, would you, sir?"

"If I were really you, I probably shouldn't. But I'm not. Are you asking my advice, Xanthias? In spite of my being your master?"

"Well, you're a God. Most folks ask their advice before an enterprise, and as you offer it free . . . You've always been decent to me in your way, that I will say, sir. Shared your dinner with me when there was trouble, and not worked me when I was sick. Now I, not being a God, can't see beyond those frogs. Except that I shall be free."

"Free, Xanthias, and I shall give you the gift of tongues into the bargain, because I don't quite know where we shall land up. I doubt if Hellas would be so pleasant as it has been up to now."

"Let's go somewhere prosperous, where there's plenty of good food and pretty girls, and singing, and lights and laughter at nights, and folk not afraid of wars!"

"I'm not sure that I can exactly manage that, Xanthias. You'd have to go a long way further on, I'm afraid. But if you're looking for prosperity and as much security as there is, we'd better trot off to England. Only I'm not sure how much of all those nice things you're going to get. After all, each of us is to go back to his own station in life."

"But I free!"

"And a citizen. That can be arranged. Well, Xanthias, you'll be set down in England with a few obols in your pocket—or whatever ridiculous coinage they aspire to. And no one is going to assert mastery over your body. No one is going to kill you or maim you or enslave you."

"That's all I ask!"

"But what about your dinner?"

"Freemen—citizens—are generous to each other."

"Well . . . I hope you'll find it so. Naturally, they could afford to be when they were a special class and not too many in it. But—yes, Xanthias?"

"What I mean to say is, Lord Dionysos, free men and citizens aren't at it all the time suspecting each other, wanting to do each other down. And I'll be able to make myself a place. A life—my own life . . . You see, sir, I've watched the guests at parties and that. They're wanting to score off each other, get each other's sweethearts p'raps. But when one's down the others'll give him a hand up. They—feel together, being citizens. Whereas a slave like me with no rights, when he's down there's no one to stand by. They laugh and give him a kick in the ribs! And the others—them that are slaves too—just because of that they don't stand by. We can't even call our pity or our courage our own. I tell you, sir, I've done that myself, seen a chap I knew laid out—no fault of his own—and never lifted a finger to help him!"

"Why not, Xanthias?"

"Afraid. Didn't know what the masters mightn't do to me for interfering. Dirty swine of a coward I was. And—that's what I meant—about manhood . . ."

"Tut tut, Xanthias, you needn't cry about it! Calm yourself, my dear boy, perhaps you'll find everything lovely the other side of Anti-Styx. Or perhaps you won't . . . Perhaps I won't either."

"Oh sir, whatever are you going to do without me? You'll never manage!"

"I think I shall manage, Xanthias; yes, I think I shall be quite comfortable. It will still be easier, even in slaveless times, for a person in my station of life to purchase service for himself."

"I don't like leaving you. Truth, I don't. You'll go getting into some mess. And who's to carry the luggage?"

"But you're going to be free, Xanthias."

"It's not what I've been accustomed to."

"Well, we needn't cross that rather unpleasant looking river. Frogs can always be ignored by the sensible person."

"But I *will* cross! Blast you, were you trying to stop me when I was all but free!"

"If you swear at me, Xanthias, I shall beat you here and now, just to show you. And you know I can hurt if I choose to exert myself . . . and use the vines and the panthers . . . No, don't look at me like that: one would think I were Medusa in person. There, boy, you'll be free in a minute and no one shall beat you. They'll only do—other things."

Brekekekex, exploit, exploit! The frogs are beginning, bulbously staring at the two climbing down the slippery bank, with a delicately godlike squeal or a proletarian grunt. Knowing there are always thistles, they have turned the donkey loose. A boat awaits. It slithers and wobbles over a heave of frogs. Brekekekex, you mutts, you mutts! Grey elephants of mist approach, circumscribe. Does the boat move still? Both banks are lost. With an injunction not to pawn, Lord Dionysos slips a ring over to Xanthias. Call me and I will come. Old companionship even of whip and chain. Brekekekex, the whip, the whip! Xanthias however accepts, feels warm, peers past mist elephants, ready and eager for all, planning new life. Dionysos Bacchos, being God, is less tense. Brekekekex, too late, too late! Now elephants part and drift trailing formlessly back to entrap new voyagers. But still the prow cuts the dangerous dark glassy waters of Anti-Styx. It seems that Xanthias is remembering forward, through the long causeless lapse of lives of other red-heads. He scowls and shifts, uneasy. There has been first for centuries slavery, the thing he knows with his own body, not changing much. Worst with Rome, then sometimes better. The slave is the soil's. The soil, once no man's, goes to kings, to barons. Runnymede not for red-heads. Brekekekex, no luck, no luck! Dead by war, plague, overwork. Churches demand souls, sometimes give help, sometimes sit back owning. With prosperity, new worlds, new markets, all shifting rise, the serfs also. Leaving the land—for what? Xanthias, as the bank nears, clenches fists, sweating. The God too seems saddened. Brekekekex, alas, for arts! The red-heads to the factories, to the looms, the mines, the foundries, mills not of God but man. The grovelling dark increase of the herded red-heads when babes are needed to tend machines. Each for himself, alcohol sole remedy. Ah Iacchos, the vines once trailing from the Acropolis . . . Brekekekex, the drink, the drink! Pubs and chapels. Xanthias looks despairingly at his master, gets no help. The stunted red-heads swarm boxed by day to work as hands for not even a known owner, by night to breed in slums. Xanthias knows all. Slack at the thwart, the frogs gobble at him. But ah here, hold up and wait, for the next memory floats up. The red-heads begin to stand together, to stand by one another. They begin to learn not to be afraid. Almost at once the machines wilt, lose grip a little. The masters come together too. All hardens. Talk in the air, thought. Brekekekex, class war, class war! Now the far bank nears, shallows slope up under the boat's keel, frogs oar away with surface flipping of wet toes. Heavy and dizzy with knowledge, hand to forehead, Xanthias steps from the boat, free. With a thin, fleeting smile, Lord Dionysos follows. The boat drifts back from their heels as though on a ferry rope. The final chorus of the frogs seeps up faintly from depths. Brekekekex, no use, no use . . .

Both now wear the dress of their station in life. Xanthias carries a bag of tools, Dionysos a smart ebony cane with golden band, presented by admirers. For him a Rolls-Royce glides, pauses, invites. He slips a hand in his pocket: there is half a crown for Xanthias. Munificent. But a film star can afford these gestures: who knows—a reporter may have seen.

The door of the Rolls-Royce closes with a discreet kiss of polish on polish. Denys Backhouse leans back with his well-known charm, crosses pale trousers, dangles a foot, taps thoughtfully on a cigarette, recedes. Ginger, the free man and citizen, picks up his tools, pockets the tip, spits after the Rolls-Royce. He knows a bit too much history to be as impressed as he should be. He starts to walk along the same road, breathing in the softly settling dust and stink of the car. His boots hurt a little, but he is used to that now.

***

There was a man standing, leaning his backside against the wall by the door where already the bricks were polished from the listless and unemployed backsides of the slump years. His name was Bill and he was intolerably unhappy because his pal Ginger was ill and, as he suspected, dying, and he could do nothing about it. From time to time he heard a cough from Ginger in bed in the front room and that tore at his guts; he had been with Ginger for an hour or two, but there wasn't anything to be done. Bill wasn't an expert at conversation with the sick, so, after they had failed to play cards at all successfully, Ginger had fretfully told Bill to clear out if he was going to look at him like a bloody girl the whole time.

Bill would have liked a fag, but he didn't have one. Wouldn't till Saturday. And if old Ginger was to get that strengthening stuff like the doctor said he ought to—well, someone had to pay for it. He kicked aimlessly at the wall, then thought of his shoes and stopped. There was nothing to think of, look at, no comfort.

A girl came out of the house and joined him. Although equally without sixpence at the moment she was considerably less unemployed than Bill, as she and her mother did all the housework; the two women had been getting through a bit of washing that morning, some of the heavy stuff, greasy overalls and that. Now she was tired and her back ached real bad. Florrie her name was. There'd been a time when she and Ginger, her mother's lodger, had wanted to get married, before he was took bad, but they hadn't been able to afford that. Not that—or anything. You can't take risks. Not these days. That was before he got the job at the brickworks that had near killed him. He oughtn't to have took it, but there was nothing doing in his own job. No, she thought, I didn't ought to have let him take it. But what's a man to do?

They stood side by side, saying nothing. Opposite each other, up and down the street, were some forty houses, exactly like the house they were leaning against. At each end the street opened into another street, exactly the same; at one corner there was a sweet shop, at the other a public house, both sad and grubby. Nothing happened. It was a bit of a walk to get to anywhere different, the park or the shops. It was a walk and then a long tram ride—if you'd got the fivepence—out to the country. Florrie and Ginger had been there twice. And now Ginger was coughing and coughing and there wasn't anything his friends could do.

A lorry passed the corner by the pub. Then a dog. Then a hand cart. Then a very large and beautiful car which glided round and so to their astonishment, and at a tap on the glass, stopped a few yards off. As the door opened Florrie flushed and gasped: "Cor lumme, Bill, it's Denys Backhouse, yes it is! I seen him in *Desert Wings*, Saturday—me and Ma went. Oh, Bill, I *know*!"

And Denys Backhouse came across the pavement and addressed them. They were dumb and staring, but after a time it penetrated to them what he was asking for. Suddenly Florrie burst into speech: "That's him coughing what you hear, sir! We put him in the front room, Ma and I did, so as he could get more air, an' the doctor said we done right, sir! He was Ma's lodger, ever so nice he was—" She began to cry. She wanted to tell it all to this stranger—this beautiful, terrible—in *Desert Wings* he'd worn a . . . what was it . . . white and soft-like round his face—but why had Ginger never said? If he was any sort of a friend of Denys Backhouse . . . Ma'd took her to the pictures, Saturday, to cheer her up, and it was the first time without Ginger. They'd used to go regular before that cough of his took a bad turn, once a week to the fourp'ny seats. And she'd cried a bit, quiet like, and then she got to looking at the story and then *he* came on—yes, she'd sat there, twisting that old-fashioned ring Ginger'd given her and sort of getting into the picture, being the heroine herself, and then sort of calling on Denys Backhouse to come and help her . . . partly to help the girl in the picture who'd been carried off by savages and partly to help Florrie whose Ginger was dying. Only then it all ended and there was a comic and they'd come back, and there was Ginger fretting about, not asleep yet . . .

Bill opened the house door and pointed to the front room. Denys Backhouse went in. The car waited, lovely-lined, shining, valuable, to be peered at and stealthily touched.

***

"Why didn't you call me earlier, Xanthias?"

"I never called you. You get out. Coming mucking round with your bleeding charity!"

"Ah . . . Xanthias, where is the ring?"

"I gave that ring to my young lady. See? And I'm through with you. See? And if you've come to get something out of me it's too late. See?"

"Don't get angry. It only makes you cough. You're not well, Xanthias."

"I'm dying, that's what. You keep your hands off me!"

"Why, Xanthias?"

"Oh, I don't care. Let 'em be. 't's all right. You aren't so bad. Bleeding parasite an' all that. How d'you like your job, anyway? Posh life I don't think!"

"Xanthias, I was the God who inspired men to frenzy and beauty and creation. Now all I can give are hollow dream-sweets, an hour's padded escape. Because of me and my art the citizens are docile and without frenzy."

"Dope, yes. Why couldn't you give us better stories?"

"It wasn't in my hands, Xanthias. I was only the artist, the one who becomes a God for the multitude. I was caught by the same thing which has caught you. I had to do what I was paid to do."

"Don't say you didn't have some choice!"

"A little, a little. And I liked the worship. Difficult, if one has been a God, to give up all that . . . I was always easy-going . . . not like Apollo and Artemis and those nasty Spartans of theirs. Besides the Company gave the public the kind of pictures it liked. If it had been offered frenzy and a new vision, would it have taken them?"

"Some of us would!"

"Not enough to pay for a modern super-production, Xanthias. And you?"

"When things were bad, I took a job in the brickyard, stoking the furnaces for the kilns. 'twasn't even Union rates . . . And I'd been a good Union man before. But the bad times killed all that, Lord Dionysos. Will it always be bad times for us red-heads whenever there's been a spell of good and we could take it easy for a moment, lift our heads, look about us?"

"That's in the hands of the red-heads, Xanthias. If you have faith . . . though what the deuce you're to have faith in . . . But perhaps Themis will wake up soon. What did they do to you at the brickyard, boy?"

"It was a sixty-five hour week and that's too much on a furnace. Dried my lungs out, it did. And my heart began to go queer and I'd no stomach for my meals. But I kept at it. And then . . . Keep your hands on me, so I don't cough. I'm fair sick of coughing."

"Do you think you are going to die, Xanthias?"

"Yes. And never marry my young lady. Nor nothing. Remember what . . . old who-was-it . . . said, takes away half a man's manhood . . ."

"That was slavery."

"You never worked me so hard as they did at the brick-kilns. Saturdays and all. And knowing all the time if I didn't keep it up, there'd be a dozen knocking themselves over to get my job. And then it would be signing on again at the Labour . . . and how they look at you when you come after a job . . . trying to kid yourself you're a man too. But you aren't. You're only a hand. If you've the luck to be that . . ."

"What shall I do for you, Xanthias?"

"The doctor said I should have port wine . . ."

"And haven't you?"

"Hell, no."

"My dear boy, that kind of miracle's child's play. There . . . And some decoration for this rather uninviting room. So. How do you like that vine? Reminds one of dear old Attica. And quite disguises the damp patches on the wall which must be a trifle uncongenial from the sick-bed . . . And some pretty little kids to nibble the lowest leaves. And an oread or two to show a leg from behind the greenery!"

"If Bill were to see that he wouldn't half laugh . . ."

"Shall we have some panthers? Gentle panthers to loop and slither round the vine stocks . . . come, my pretties . . . it's dark and cool here under the vine, but outside there's sun bright and hot and the quartz pebbles sparkling . . . What is it you hear, Xanthias?"

"Lord Dionysos, I hear the frogs. Lift me a little, put your arm behind me . . . be with me to the brink . . . Dionysos Anikete."

Brekekekex, come back, come back . . . It is not every slave whose master tends him to the bank, to Charon's ferry-boat. Charon tips his forelock to Dionysos, recognising a major Immortal. Yes, he will take particular care of this passenger. Yes, he looks somewhat over tired. Brekekekex, to sleep, to sleep . . . Xanthias sits in the boat. He is not coughing any longer. He is not bothered by thoughts of his young lady or any eternally postponed epithalamion. He is not afraid or angry or anxious about his job. The boat pushes off silently through the goggling golden eyes, the spring-green humped backs, the webbed water-fingers. Brekekekex, good-bye, good-bye . . .

Thus it was that Bill and Florrie, peeping round the corner of the door, discovered that Ginger had tactlessly and in the most inconsiderate manner for one in his station of life, died in the arms of the great film star. It was something for Florrie to tell the reporters about, something beautiful and soothing and comforting. Dignity and importance had come to the house for the first time in its history. Their shadow made Florrie, who had genuinely loved her Ginger, for a time beautiful and romantic. So in the end, and with the help of press photographers, it was better for her than if she had married the man she loved.

But Denys Backhouse took Bill aside and said: "Where is this brickyard? For it's my opinion it killed Ginger."

Bill said heavily: "That's what I say, sir. But you can't get anything out of the insurance . . . Christ, I wish I could get at the bastard that owns it!"

"Who is the . . . gentleman?"

"Bleeder of the name of Thompson. Pays Union rates in the yard when he's got to, but the minute he can get round them, like on the furnace work, he does."

"That is not unusual, Bill . . . may I call you Bill? I suggest that we proceed to the brickyard and interview Mr. Thompson."

"What—about Ginger? *He* won't do nothing. And we can't. And old Ginger's dead, blast him! And some other poor bastard'll get his job and get done in the same way."

"I'm not so sure. Come into my car, Bill. So."

At a touch the engine woke, the wheels glided forward, glided past the corner, for ever out of the street. Bill sat forward on the seat, cap in hands, feet together, aware in contrast with the sleek cushioned and shining car, that he was grubby, ugly, inferior, that his boots were through at the toe, that he was wearing a ragged muffler instead of the collar and tie a Rolls-Royce demands. All this enhanced his misery. And he would never be able to laugh about it with Ginger—Ginger so good at laughing at toffs! Ginger lying there queer and still, not coughing, not answering back. Ginger finished, done in, dead. He wiped his eyes with his cap, hoping Mr. Backhouse wouldn't notice. And Mr. Backhouse leant back well used to softness and glitter, but his eyes appeared peculiarly black and hard and his lips had tight muscles pressed round them. And so they arrived at Mr. Thompson's brickyard, and Bill cautiously, cap in hand, followed the great film star out of the Rolls-Royce.

Mr. Thompson himself came to interview such a potential customer, beaming with class-servility. He was a very ordinary man, no special villain. He regretted the death of his employee, but such things cannot be blamed upon working conditions. No doubt the man was constitutionally unfitted for such work. Long hours? The industry demanded them. It was impossible to run a brickyard in any other way. These were hard times and if he was unable to make any profits he would have to close down and then where would his workmen be! Anyway, this was a free country, the man had accepted the conditions and the wages. They hadn't been forced on him, and he needn't have taken the job if he hadn't wanted it! And as for you, sir, if you've come to my yard not as an honest customer but a meddling busybody, I'll thank you to clear out!

Mr. Backhouse swung his gold-mounted cane: "Those, I take it, are the kilns whose furnaces killed your employee?"

"You clear out of my yard this instant or I'll have the police in!"

Bill flinched, but not Denys Backhouse, who had never had occasion to fear the police. He waved the cane once more. Something peculiar seemed to be happening to the kilns. The bricks in the walls were bulging. Three or four dropped out with a loud, disconcerting noise. Bill stayed very still, crouched a little, twisting his cap in his hands, breathing chokily. Where the bricks had dropped out a vine was growing with great rapidity, crawling up and down, loosening more and more bricks, bulging into lewd, mocking grapes. Mr. Thompson sat down abruptly, on nothing. Nobody even laughed. There were other vines pushing the brickyard about. They shoved the neat baked piles crashing. They rippled leafily along. The foreman and half a dozen men were watching, eyes and mouths open. One of the vines plucked at a man's leg; he swore violently and bolted; the others followed. The vine pulled over a couple of wheelbarrows. The face of Mr. Denys Backhouse was intent and pleased. The brick kilns were all in ruins now. Out of the ruins delicately stepped a panther, then two. Mr. Thompson crawled rapidly towards Mr. Denys Backhouse, hatless, earthy, squeaking in an unpleasant way. The gold-mounted cane, waved once, held him in position, scrabbling. The panthers approached with snarls and greedy tail-twitches.

Bill said, in a loud and sudden voice: "You can't go doing *that*, sir, not even if the whole bloody thing's a bloody dream!"

"Why not?" asked Mr. Denys Backhouse, but gestured the panthers flat.

"Because—" Bill began, "because—what's the good of it?"

"I think we agreed that this gentleman who is about to have his throat bitten out by my panthers, virtually murdered Ginger. I think, don't you, it would be nice to do justice for that murder."

"No," said Bill, "I don't, and I won't have it! Ginger was my pal. We done things together. Agreed he was as good as murdered. But this isn't going to make him alive, so what's the use, I ask you, what's the use?"

"It might stop other owners of brickyards from making the same bargain with other men who are out of work and have no choice. Don't you think so, Bill?"

"No I don't, and it's not sense. Killing one man won't alter nothing, an' he's no worse than the rest. It would be only—accidental-like. It's not just brickyards, neither, the whole blasted thing's wrong, and it'll take more than you to put it right even if you was God almighty!"

"You refuse, then, to allow this man's death, even though Ginger—"

"You lay your tongue off of Ginger, though I say it to your face, sir, whoever you are! Ginger and me, that's finished. And I'm the only one knows about it now. And this won't help and it's not what I'm used to and what we need is Unions for all and all in the Unions! And we aren't killing anyone, least of all so bloody casual!"

"Suppose my panthers clawed him a little? . . . not to death?"

"It's not *English!*" said Bill, white to the lips now, and his hands had twisted all the lining out of his cap, "and it's not going to do no good!"

With that, Mr. Denys Backhouse waved his cane once more and the panthers stalked away and disappeared among the foliage, and even that wilted and withered and vanished. But the kilns were down and the brick piles overset, and their owner was still grovelling in the mud. Yet now again he was beginning to murmur words about the police.

"Come along, Bill," said Mr. Denys Backhouse, "the car is waiting." Bill stumbled after him and into the car, not conscious now of shine or softness. By this time Mr. Thompson had crawled to knee-height and was shaking both fists after them. Again the Rolls-Royce drew away. "Where can I drop you, Bill?" asked the film star, flicking a morsel of lime from his trouser-leg. And added: "What do you propose doing now?"

Bill said: "I'm on the dole. It's all one to me. Christ, I'm tired! Them bloody brutes."

"I could offer you a job," said his companion slowly.

"Could you, sir? A tempor'y job, like?"

"No, permanent. Ginger's old job, as a matter of fact."

"He never said . . ."

"I can imagine that he wouldn't. Yet it was a nice job in a way. Compared with his last. But you would lose your freedom, Bill."

"Freedom. What for?"

"Oh. To vote and all that."

"There's a lot o' firms where they don't like you voting Labour. Dunno that I care much. Not if it's a decent job."

"And you'd have to ask before you got married." "That's so in some firms. But if it's a decent job—"

"And you wouldn't get any regular wages. But you'd get food and lodging . . . and a good deal of fun. And if you were ill you'd get looked after."

"But—Who are you, anyway, sir?"

"I happen to be the God Dionysos Bacchos. An Immortal. The God of divine frenzy. By the way, would you like a drink?"

"I could do with one, sir . . . And this job?"

"Your pal Ginger was my slave."

"But that's not . . . legal."

"It is where I come from and would take you. Oh, ever so legal. Would you mind being my slave?"

"'twouldn't be so different from now. Wage-slaves, that's us. In a manner of speaking. Ginger, he used to say so. In a nasty kind of way, if you take me, as though he'd been expecting something else. Which there isn't. Not for the likes of us. Not yet. And so he gets done in. Christ, I got bloody fond of old Ginger an' his talk!"

Bill bowed his head in his hands. Mr. Denys Backhouse lighted a cigarette and watched the even flowing-by of houses; now they were passing through suburban acres of villa and small garden; above none showed any Acropolis. He observed at last: "Do you agree, then, to come?"

"I dunno," said Bill. "Why didn't Ginger never mention you, like?"

"It's apt to be rather difficult, mentioning the Gods."

"You are a God—straight?"

"Yes."

"Then—when it come to them panthers—why did you do what I said? You didn't need to have—not if you was a God. You might have set them to killing me."

"I'm not above taking advice. Besides, was your affair primarily, as Ginger's friend. I once did something of the same kind with some pirates, but it was my affair then. I'll tell you all about it if you come with me. In any event, ideas change; no one questioned my action in regard to the pirates, some of whom I killed and some of whom I turned into dolphins; but that was some time ago. Bill, do you believe I'm a God?"

"Yes."

"Coming?"

"It don't seem right, somehow, once having run across a God—which I haven't up till now, for all they give me liquorice sticks at Sunday school—to turn him down. But then—what about Rule Britannia and all that?"

"Do you call yourself a free man now, Bill? Are you able freely to create and wander and think and love?"

"Hell, no."

"Coming?"

"Yes."

The car now had passed through the suburbs, out into the country, beyond the tram stops, beyond the hikers' rambling-spots, beyond anything Bill had ever known. Ahead lay a large river, planting itself down across England without leave of atlases. And Bill began to hear the croaking of the chorus of frogs.

THE FURIES DANCE IN NEW YORK

So we said, where shall we find the loveliest thing in New York?
And some said in Fifth Avenue or Fifty-seventh Street, and
    some said
In the Socialist Party, or, as they were mostly highbrows,
In the Communist Party. And what about Radio City?
And what about Manhattan Bridge and what about . . . ?
But we were already slinking off,
Finding the voices a trifle difficult, feeling a little browbeaten,
    having been told that England
Is dead and decaying, her culture rotten from its class basis up,
Or having been told, still worse, that England is marvellous,
The one place that will be left standing in a chaotic world
(Like an exhibit of a stage coach and two crinolines).
So, as I said, nickel in fist, we had slunk off into the El.

Here in the Natural History Museum, having dodged the
    meteorites
Which God the mathematician for some odd reason saw fit
To strew like Xs over Kansas (X equals nothing),
We have come to the Indian section. The Indians, as everyone
    knows,
Are being assimilated, that is the Good Indians
Who go to the Church schools and learn to sell things and be
    customers themselves.

The Bad Indians were all killed by the ancestors of the Christian
    Scientists,
The ancestors of the Rotarians, the readers of Esquire, and the
    D.A.R.,
The ancestors of Franklin D. Roosevelt, General Johnson and
    Huey Long.
What the hell anyway. The Bad Indians were killed.
And a good job too.

This Indian pottery is more beautiful than anything in Fifth
    Avenue,
If it had been made to-day in a studio, on some fresh
    inspiration,
People would be going crazy over it, the art critics and the
    highbrows;
It would be sold for large sums to Park Avenue, but the Com-
    munists also
Would tell us it was authentic.
This Indian basket work, this exquisite feathering,
This accurate bloom of colour, this patterned certainty,
Precariously preserved in a few glass cases, it is astonishing, I
    think,
Do you not think so?

Citizens of New York, flock round in reverence.
Could you have made these things? No. No fear. Jeez, no!
What can you make, citizens? They answer, look at us.
Look at us!

We are unskilled labour,we can turn wheels, press handles, put
    salted nuts in bags,
But we can't make anything.
Citizens, citizens, your fathers made ploughshares, made
    ox-yokes,
Your mothers embroidered linen shirts, in Dalmatia, in Italy,
In Greece, in Portugal, in Poland, Hungary, Latvia,
What have you done with the skill of your fathers and mothers?
What have you done with their patterns?

But the citizens shake their heads, not comprehending all this:
Our fathers and mothers were dumb: who wants ox-yokes,
Who wants embroidered shirts? Woolworths don't stock them,
    huh?
Our fathers and mothers, they got quit of that on Ellis Island.
We got nothing. We want nothing. See?

Let us return to the glass cases, to the difficult contemplation of
    beauty
That was being made in this continent three centuries ago,
That was of value for the world, for mankind, for all these
    abstractions
Which somehow we believe in (although no doubt
We shall be told they are the results of a class education
At places like Oxford, England.)
And this civilisation was shot up, destroyed, ended,
Lost for the world and mankind. Lost, all that it might have
    turned into.
Lost. Lost.

People who destroy things are apt to get a curse on them.
We should have observed this often enough in history
(Only history is dumb stuff, as Henry Ford said, bunk)
To have realised its necessity. No use trying to escape
Once you've destroyed something the gods loved, destroyed
    something
That should have been eternal. No use, the Furies get after you.
Pretty soon, boy, they'll have you down
And rip your guts out.

And it isn't much of a step from shooting Indians
To shooting strikers. It isn't much of a step
From exterminating the Indian civilisation to exterminating
Your own.

And who will weep on the grave, who will put Fifth Avenue
In a glass case? Who will be there to contemplate? Only the
    Furies
In their black shirts and red shirts, dancing the Horst Wessel
    Carmagnole?
Will they be there? Or nothing?

Or is it possible
That a few Indians may come back, slowly, out of the
    Reservations,
Out of the Pueblos, smiling a little, a little,
Stretching their arms a little, looking about them a little?
And they will begin putting things in order, letting the decent
    earth

And the decent rivers eat up what they will, letting iron rust
And concrete crumble, and the old bodies of Fords
Be grown over quietly with brambles where in time will nest
Oriole and cardinal.
And they will dance the rain dances and bring back the rain
To the parched deserts which the settlers' ploughing made
Out of the buffalo lands. And they will watch the forest
    growing,
Slowly and softly growing on the eroded mountain sides,
Till the top soil comes back. And there will be no newspapers
To eat the forests. And there will be no advertisements
On the trunks of the forest trees. And the Indians will move
    quietly
About the forests, with their minds full of patterns.
And there is no doubt they will be a hundred per cent
American . . .

GRAND-DAUGHTER

(For Stella Benson and *The House of Living Alone*)

Last week I was looking through some of the political books of the nineteen-thirties. It is queer reading those old books now, careful, angry, unhappy books in hard red covers with sad black lettering. All the authors, with their prefaces and tables of statistics and careful indexes, speak of the new times which they tried to foresee, as though it would all make a great difference to people; but they never saw what kind of a difference it was going to be. Most of the people who wrote those books were economists, poor things, or else a special sort of historian which existed then, who was trained to see just one particular kind of event, like a truffle-pig. And those who were capable of seeing other sorts of events such as we can see now (Brailsford for instance) were rather ashamed of this side of their minds. There were also, of course, the physicists and to some extent the biologists and biochemists, though the latter were usually humbler, having rather less immediate contact with the technocrats and a good deal of sympathy, because of their manual technique, with the factory workers.

My grandfather on my mother's side must have read dozens of these books; he even wrote one or two. They must have affected him considerably. I take it they made people gloomy and over intent on that side of life, and must have made them feel inferior and changeable compared with the figures and statistics which strode about over their heads. I should have hated living then!

Yet I expect my grandfather believed in it all, or at any rate thought there was no other kind of thing which could better be believed in.

His wife, my grandmother, was very much laughed at for saying that the industrial revolution had destroyed magic. She was of course a Marxist, as most of them were, and preferred seeing things in economic terms. It was plain to her that play of any kind must have been exceedingly ill-thought-of in the moral system of a ruling class which had made its position by making other people work for it, and, to some extent, by working itself. Magic was one step beyond play. And so the whole idea of magic had become immoral—it had in fact arrived at the stage of immorality where people cease altogether to believe in a thing—and serious, moral people such as socialists did not use the word at all. But my grandmother managed to use it to herself, and she could at least see in a kind of apologetic, theoretical way, that good magic, being essentially democratic, could not work itself out in a pyramidal society of haves on a basis of have-nots, but must at best go underground and at worst turn into something evil and individual and undemocratic.

It was rare for anyone to see even that much. Most people were hopelessly under the sway of the economists and the early technocrats. So, when my grandmother once said that she wanted socialism so as to set magic free, they all laughed at her. But yet she did not wholly believe in it herself. She must have felt that it was the same thing as the Good Life, which is of course only half the truth.

My grandparents on the other side presumably did not even read the gloomy old books, or very rarely; in general they were too tired and under-fed and ignorant to read much unless it had been predigested for them. Still, perhaps they read bits of them sometimes. It's hard to picture at all how they lived; one has to make a great effort and find the right sympathetic formulæ before one can begin to understand their lives. However, it is quite worthwhile doing. Then one can arrive at the crushing dullness of their routine of existence and their consequent inability to look forward at change. Those two other grandparents of mine were both Labour Party members, as they called it, which meant in a way that they wanted new times to come, yet they never thought of these new times as being different in detail from what had already been experienced.

Yes, I suppose it all happened curiously differently from any way that anyone in, say, the nineteen thirties, supposed. None of them foresaw the technocrats, not at least with anything like accuracy. Still less did they foresee how the final cracking-up of the pyramid would happen. I expect they were all so dried-up and unhappy and resentful that they had to see it wrong. I very much doubt, even, whether many of them had the sense to be happy when it did come—but so differently from their intentions. Perhaps they'd all been longing for the chance to hit back, poor dears, for themselves or others, and of course there was none of that.

Probably even someone like my mother's mother was deeply surprised when, for instance, the dancing started. She used to dance as a young woman—or so one gathers from old letters—but as she grew older and more involved, so that kind of thing dropped out of her way of life. Any dancing which she or her husband might have taken part in was the curious individual dancing of the epoch, in which couples crossed and crossed one another's pattern or purpose and each one of a couple could be separate in thought and feeling, even without pleasure. It seems so plain now, that no sensible person ought to have been astonished at the connection between the new democracy and the great patterns of dancing that spread out from London and Birmingham, but yet it appears that they were.

One takes all these things for granted so much that it is hard to think oneself back to their viewpoint. The fundamental which they never saw is, I take it, the plain fact (given the nature of the Universe) that if one thing is altered everything is altered. It only remains to discover the key thing or things; but these are sometimes so apparently incongruous that educated people used to dislike taking them seriously. No doubt in the very old days, magic—for why not stick to a good word?—was practised by men and women who did not know what they were doing, often did something else by mistake, and were anyway frightened of the possibilities of their own technique. The early evidence is proof of this. As magic, with the decline of even agricultural equality, came unstuck from its place in society, so the practisers of magic came to be unsocial or anti-social persons, and by the end of the nineteenth century "magic," such as it was, had mainly got into the hands of a particularly nasty type of person, with whom decent members of society would not associate, and whom they could not trust to tell the truth.

Besides this there was, during my grandmother's time, another thing which worried people. I wonder if I can explain it! Historically, it seems clear, their morality had become increasingly rationalist—due no doubt very largely to the instruments of precision of the late nineteenth and early twentieth century; but that is neither here nor there. They were very proud and anxious about this rationalism of theirs, which was still a symbol of their only recent freeing from the primitive (though of course not really earliest) tyrannies of kings by divine right and the various organised priesthoods and religions. All intelligent, forward-thinking people, even in the so-called imaginative professions, insisted on the recognition of their rationality and put it constantly into their talk and writing. If they had not done so, they would have been ashamed to face their own technocrats and economists! Yet, of course, that was not the whole of life. They would naturally not allow the other side to be pointed out to them by priests; but occasionally a doctor, and very rarely some writer whom they trusted, was allowed to do so. But the difficulty was that they saw this other side taking shape in several comic, but extremely unpleasant and dangerous, group madnesses, such as that which affected the Fascists in Italy or the Nazis in Germany. What they did not, apparently, realise, was that the Nazi irrationality—or perhaps anti-technocracy?—was only successful because it gave some solid fulfilment to a definite need in human beings. The rationalists stupidly feared and hated this need (exactly as an earlier generation feared and hated other kinds of needs in human beings) and refused to satisfy it decently and creatively. Yet, if in the end the new thing had not happened, had not, as it were, cracked and pushed up through the unencumbered soil of democracy and equality, this evil reflection of the other side might well have lasted for generations, instead of dying out as rapidly and completely as it actually did in Germany and elsewhere.

It seems very odd that a woman like my grandmother could not have seen this clearly and plainly and been able to explain it convincingly to her generation! Was she in some way ashamed? Or could she just not quite believe in it? Presumably, until it happened, it could only be a hypothesis. All she could hope to say with any conviction was: there may be going to be something of this kind, if we can make a set of circumstances which will allow it to happen. And then, of course, she got so involved in making the set of circumstances (which meant, for her at least, taking political action towards equality) that she could not keep her eyes open, even, for the small signs which must have been apparent, of the kind of life which was about to come. If she had been less involved in the making of those circumstances and more able to look, it would have meant that she cared less for the idea of change. And at least I am certain of one thing: that she *did* care.

As to my other grandmother on my father's side, she didn't have time to think at all, poor darling. When people talked to her on her doorstep about equality and democracy, or rather about "the triumph of the Labour Party," she pictured a secure job for her husband, cheap food and shelter, and perhaps less hard work for herself. She never seems to have considered the possibility of happiness. And so when it came she found she couldn't quite accept it. There must be something wrong, some catch. I can remember her old, wrinkled face, always full of a kind of surprised disapproval which I couldn't understand at all until I began learning history and became aware of the generations of misery taken for granted, which had made those eyes and mouth. She outlived my other grandparents; a working woman was bound to be pretty tough, and she'd been that for forty years.

Yes, it must have been terrible living then, in that hopelessness of any real difference, with that sense of being stuck which must have oppressed them all. When it was all going to be—not easy, but at any rate, simple. As we, now, have come, through our well-wishing of those before us, to understand.

THE FANCY PIG

There used to be a pig on Princes Risborough hill:
A fat white sow on the road, lying quite still.
Every time I went there, and most of all at night,
I thought I should see that pig in my yellow headlight.
But every time, at the top, there had been no pig there,
Only beech hedges in the cool, waiting air,
Only leaves stirring in the dark air's flow,
And this time again my Thing had let me go.

What was the pig of mine, this fancy pig,
With light hairs on her hams, and her udders big?
Was she once a real sow in a Bucks farm-yard,
Then pork, ham, trotters, pig's fry and lard?
Or was she something in me which I so needed to kill
That I had to grow her a body on Princes Risborough hill?
Or was she something else that was neither me nor her
But a stray twist of fancy on a chalk road's blur?

For all I know, she may be lying there still,
Waiting these seven years on Princes Risborough hill.
For I never go there now, by day nor yet by night,
With clutch and brakes and steering, and yellow headlight;
I never go there now, where often I have been,
The long beech-twigs lightly brushing my wind-screen.
But some other woman, with pigs in her to kill,
May have run down my fancy sow on Princes Risborough hill.

THE SNOW MAIDEN

Once again the Snow Maiden was born, the daughter of January and April. Once again she was hated by the sun-god, the man-god, the god of life and potency. Once again, for her safety, her parents sent her to live amongst the mortals.

She was boarded out at five shillings a week by the Poor-law authorities, and her name was Mary Snow. She was pretty enough to eat, blue eyes and curly hair, as yellow and shiny as a Caution Stop, whenever her foster-mother—Mrs. Smith her name was—a good old sort, and so was her man, Mr. Smith, a tram-driver for the Corporation—whenever she'd time to help Mary give it a wash. At school everyone liked Mary Snow, and some of the big girls were always wanting to baby her up, but she wasn't having any. There'd been a bit of a fuss about her scholarship, her being a Poor-law kid and all, but her school teachers kicked up no end of a bother till she got it all right. Clever she was, too, and most of all with what's not common in a girl, and that's mathematics. The teachers used to talk her over with one another over their lunches, and they all said they'd never seen anything like it.

And she was prettily spoken, though where she picked it up, no one knew, for the Smiths were just plain folks in a back street in Aston, and that's no beauty-spot, as everyone in Birmingham knows, or would if they took a No 8 from the centre, the line Mr. Smith used to drive on. But where she did get her pretty way of speaking from was her mother, her real one, that used to come into her room of a night in Spring-time—down through the sky-light, for Mary's room was just a bit of a corner that had been a box-room in old days when the place had been a one-family house and servants kept. She'd sit on the end of Mary's bed, would that April, looking for all the world like a young girl, not an old married woman—or what you might call married, for I never heard that her and old January ever went to church, the way decent folks do in Birmingham and elsewhere.

She'd sit there, chattering half the night to Mary, and all round them the room'd be full of the scents and flowers and bird-songs and sunrises that had slipped in after her through the skylight, fidgety little things they were, all legs and eyes and wings, perching on the edge of the Co-op calendar, and scuttering up and down Mary's old macintosh on the door-peg, and when they'd gone they'd leave a kind of a dancy, crazy feeling behind them, that'd go on into Mary's dreams. But she never told Mrs. Smith, though she was fond enough of her in a way, and she never told her teachers, nor any of the girls at school, not even Betty Wothers, who was a council scholar and ever so good at languages and history, and she never told any of the boys who came round after her and took her to the movies, evenings, or a shilling tram-ride out on to the Lickeys of a Sunday.

For she had the boys all round her, had Mary, from the time she was fifteen, and some of them steady chaps with a good job, the marrying kind, working full time at Cadbury's, as it might be, or the Birmingham Small Arms. Any other girl would have got silly, I know I would have, but Mary didn't. She knew what was what, maybe she got that from her mother, and she didn't ever let them get messing around with her, no, not even coming back from the Lickeys of a summer night, when it's been sweet and cool up there among the trees, but then you get down near the tram-stop, and it's warmer, and you get out the Gold-flakes and light up, and there's a smell from the public houses that are opening now and your boy says Let's have one, and you hear the girls and young fellows larking and giggling about, and there's the Bristol Road ahead of you all dipping and lifting and shining with lights and traffic—well, you know. But Mary didn't care, she just nipped up on a tram, and if the boys wanted to stay with her—and you bet they did—they had to nip up too.

There was only one boy she liked at all, and when you got down to it all she really liked about Bert Hobbis was that he was a mathematician too. Believe it or not, those two used to go off of a Sunday, talking nineteen to the dozen, and when you listened it was nothing but a pack of nonsense about coefficients and absolutes and I don't know what-all. Bert was a nice-looking young fellow, too, and sometimes he'd want a kiss at the end of all that mathematics, but he didn't get it, or at least, not the way a young fellow likes to get a kiss from a pretty girl. Mary wanted the talk well enough to give him just what would keep him quiet, but that was all.

And so things went on till she was near seventeen, and it seemed like she was sure to get a scholarship at the University. Everyone was talking about it down Aston way. But then a fellow came along. He was a traveller from Manchester, in cotton goods, and the last time he'd been along he'd been walking out with Mary's friend, Betty Wothers, and they were as good as fixed up. He'd got a lot of connections, and he was a big, red-faced chap with curly black hair, sort of foreign type, not Lancashire at all, and as strong as a horse; why he could lift a fifty pound box of samples as easy as wink. Well, this time, when he was waiting about at the corner by the Feathers for Betty, who should come along but Mary Snow, as pretty as a picture and all by herself.

Well, there are some who said it was her fault, there always are when it's a girl. But I say, she wasn't that sort, it wasn't in her then, not if she'd wanted to. But whether or no, this young fellow—his name was George Higginson—he just up and followed her, and when she'd got a bit past the turning, he stepped up to her and said Good evening, Miss, and the next minute he'd got both arms round her and was squeezing her up like the bad men on the movies. Mary let out one screech, and do you know what happened then? Why, a crowd of birds flew into his face, sparrows they must have been for there's nothing else in Aston, and he said afterwards he felt like as if he was being slashed about with branches and prickles. Anyway, he let Mary go, and she went tearing off home, and she never told anyone, least of all Betty Wothers.

But Betty got to know. Oh yes! That George Higginson went straight round to her house, just like a man, and he said: "We aren't going to get married. See?" Just like that he said it, for she told me so herself, and then there was a nice turn-up, what with Betty screeching and her mother going all red and dignified and getting the words mixed up, and him telling them both off—oh real nasty, he was, and he said he was going to marry Mary Snow and no other girl, no, not if all the girls in Aston came along on their bended knees, and that was that!

Well then, it was all over the place and everyone set on Mary, like they would. But she said: "I'm not having any of that from him. He's not going to sell *me* any samples!" And you saw she really meant it like that. Some thought she was just kidding, but I didn't. I knew she came all over queer when a man got hold of her that way, felt like she was melting, she said. She'd get real frightened, and she couldn't get it out of her head except by studying in her school books, that were getting more and more difficult and full of outlandish looking figures and squiggles. She shut herself up now in her attic, and studied for her scholarship, and when young George Higginson's thick red lips and curly hair came back on her—you know, like onions—she got up and scrubbed her face with cold water and went on at her books and figuring.

Well, after that, three things happened. Young George had half a ticket in the sweep and won £100, and Betty's mother, Mrs. Wothers, took it into her head that Betty ought to sue him for breach. That was one. But Betty wouldn't, and why? Because Bert Hobbis, the boy who was keen on mathematics, had got a job as draughtsman at Austin's, and he got keen on Betty, and she got keen on him, and pretty soon they were walking out regular. That was two. And then old Mrs. Smith began going on at Mary about how she ought to be a bit nice to George Higginson, who was always hanging about the place whenever he was in Birmingham, and who'd bought a scarf and a 2 lb. box of chocs for Mary out of his sweep money; Mrs. Smith kept on hinting how useful that £100 would come in, and how she'd always treated Mary as a real daughter—which was true enough. That was three.

Mary, poor kid, took it a bit hard. She couldn't get away from Mrs. Smith nagging and hinting, not even when she was sitting over her books, for the old woman had got all worked up over the £100 and what a chance it was for Mary. But when she went out there was plenty of neighbours ready to say something spiteful, as if it had been her fault. She let on she didn't care, but of course she did, and they noticed at school that she wasn't as careful over her work as she had been. Most of the boys wanted to take her out still, though some were beginning to be a bit impatient, saying you never got anywhere with such a stuck-up kid, and they were a bit afraid of what George Higginson might do—if he saw another fellow hanging round Mary, he'd go for them like a bull. Anyway, Mary didn't want to go out with fellows, no more than she used to; she just wasn't made that way. She did want to go talking mathematics with Bert Hobbis, but that was n.b.g. now; he spent all his evenings with Betty, and he didn't seem somehow so taken up with mathematics as he was. Not that I could ever see what either of them saw in it.

There were times Mary got her home-work finished early and then she'd go out for a walk before bed-time, and sometimes she used to see Betty and Bert together, walking home, as it might be, and his arm round her and her head snuggling down on his shoulder, both looking soft and solemn, the way two of you do when he's got a steady job and prospects, and you're both thinking about getting a little house and a bit of garden somewhere on the new estates, and you're thinking about all the things that never seemed worth thinking about before—rates and rent and gas cookers, and wallflower and broccoli plants for bedding— and he says: "I put our names down on the list for a Council house"—and you say: "Mum's going to fix us up for crockery and I was looking through the sales catalogues"—and then you pass a shop with baby clothes and woolly lambs, and you look at one another and both of you giggle a bit and look away, and it's made you feel all soft and silly like you never thought you could be, only now it seems all right somehow. That was how Bert and Betty were.

And, you see, Mary didn't understand—well, no one does till they've had the chance themselves, but Mary, she understood less than most. Only, she could make out well enough that they were happy, and that they didn't want to talk to her. Two or three evenings she'd seen them that way, and the last evening she'd watched them ten minutes and more, both standing staring in at Lewis' window, looking at curtain stuffs, and Betty saying she'd seen just as good down Aston way at half the price—the way one does, you know, when one wants something bad but one hasn't the money for it. And Mary could hear the way they talked to one another, not minding a bit about things they couldn't get, not minding anything yet, just because they were in love. And Betty Wothers was never once thinking of school days with Mary and how keen they'd both got about class-work and hockey on Saturdays, and doing better than the rest of the girls, and having tea with the headmistress. And Bert forgetting all about his mathematics and the ambitions he used to say he had—not about getting on at the Works, like he was always telling Betty he was going to, but about being a great professor at the University and all that. Well, of course they weren't thinking of any such thing now, neither of them! But Mary, she just couldn't understand, she couldn't get it straight in her head that men and women do just fall in love with one another and then they don't care any more about their friends nor what they used to want to do and be. It's plain enough to most of us, or how would the world go on, but it wasn't plain to Mary Snow.

So Mary, she just turned and went back, walking rather quick so that she wouldn't get spoken to at the corner of the Arcade or in Corporation Street. It took her a bit of time getting home, and instead of thinking about mathematics the way she mostly did when she was alone, she kept on puzzling and fidgeting about Betty and Bert, wondering what it was that made them look like that and act like that. It made her feel lonely, and a bit cold, somehow, and then she began remembering young George Higginson and how it had felt when he'd caught hold of her and squeezed her up. And because she'd hated that and because she remembered pretty clear just exactly the way she'd hated it, she felt lonelier than ever, and a bit frightened. She got home all right, and said good-night quickly and went to her little room, up the stairs where the lino was mostly worn away and the plaster was a bit loose here and there, the way it is in old houses. She sat down on the bed, carefully, because there was one of the iron legs of the frame that was a bit funny, and she hunched herself up with her outdoor coat still on and the counterpane round her shoulders on top of that, and she began reading one of her books on mathematics.

But it didn't help her this time. It didn't stop her feeling lonely. It didn't make those nice comfortable, five-way patterns come up in her mind, the way she liked. It didn't somehow seem to make sense. She'd kicked off her shoes and was wriggling her stocking-feet up against one another to get warm; her hands were cold too and she tucked them one at a time under her armpits hoping they'd warm up soon; she didn't mind being cold really, not like some—mostly she worked better so. But it was all nothing to how cold her mind was: it was just as though there wasn't anything in the world would ever be able to warm it up again.

So she began to write marks on a piece of paper, the same as if she'd been figuring out one of those kind of examples you get in the Advanced, and she wrote out some long numbers, with decimal places in them and all that, and she put them together into sums. Only they were a queer kind of sum, and while she was doing that she kept on talking to herself. And when it was all finished and cancelled out, her mother came down through the skylight, her mother April, all in a dazzle of pale sparkly sunshine, with trimmings of green like what you always forget in winter, and then one Sunday you take a bus-ride off into the country, and it's all new, newer than your new Spring hat, so new and clean and surprised looking, if you see what I mean, that you don't hardly like to touch the grass under the bushes or the silly little beech leaves all beginning again. It was the same as that with April, she didn't look as though she ought to be touched. But all the same, oh she was kind and sweet and gentle, and Mary shut her eyes and snuggled up against her, and she felt like her feet were treading in soft warm moss and her hands were spread out in the sun, and "Mother," she said, "Oh Mother, I want what Bert and Betty's got!"

Then April's face, it got all still and solemn, like the last minute before a rain-storm, and she said: "You remember about the Sun."

"Yes," said Mary. "I remember and I don't care. I won't go on just being Snow.'"

And April said again: "You have to decide, but if you choose wrong, it will be too late afterwards."

But Mary said: "I've got to understand. It spoils everything if I don't know this. Once and for all, Mother, I have chosen. Make me understand. Give me what they've got. I don't want to be different any longer."

And April said: "I can't keep it from you now. You have chosen." And there were tears in her eyes, as it might be great still raindrops on the end of a pussy willow bough before you break it off to take home. But Mary didn't see that.

And then all sorts of things came edging along and getting at Mary. Pretty things mostly: primroses and cowslips and lambs and that, and misty soft mornings and evenings like you'd feel all mazed in, hearing bells from somewhere at the back of the elm trees: and little brown bubbly streams coming down between ferns; and the first cuckoo and the first tulips, and the last of the big daffodils: and plum blossom like you see it on each side of the Bromsgrove Road going down into Worcestershire, and blue sky and little white clouds, and split-sticky chestnut buds. And some of the things weren't exactly pretty, but they got at her all the same, things, you know, like frogs in a pool, croaking like mad and messing and heaving about in the dirty water till you don't know which way to look, hardly—Well, there they were, all April's creatures let loose on Mary Snow. And by and bye she let go her hold on her mother and she lay back, smiling a bit, and the next morning she woke up in bed but she couldn't remember how she'd got undressed, and when she tried to remember she began to giggle, all by herself under the bed-clothes. And when she got up she didn't once look at her books, but she spent the best part of half an hour trying to fix her hair a new way, like she'd seen in an advertisement in the *Herald*. And she was late for school the first time for months.

Her teacher didn't scold her, because she'd got so used to Mary being the best in the class, but she got a bit worried because all morning Mary didn't seem to be attending the way she'd always done before, and she'd have been more worried if she'd known that Mary was thinking about that young traveller, George Higginson, and how he was due back in Birmingham that day. It was queer for Mary, because she could still remember how she used to think about him, but she didn't think like that any longer. She was wanting him to take her to the pictures and her to sit next him, and she knew already somehow just how she'd let him know by sitting a bit closer—and how his hand would come creeping over onto her knee, creeping under the edge of her frock—Well, that wasn't what she ought to have been thinking at school, not about a young fellow that had given another girl the chuck, but still, one can't blame her. Most girls would be like that with that kind of a mother.

Next day she told Mrs. Smith that she and George Higginson were going to get married the end of the month. Mrs. Smith was as pleased as Punch; she thought it was her doing. They weren't so pleased at the school, for it meant an end to all the scholarship plans. The head mistress had her up and gave her a talking to, telling her what a fine thing it would be for her to go to the University, trying to get her all worked up about it like she used to be. But Mary just stood there, grinning a bit, looking as pretty as ever but somehow very aggravating for the head mistress, and all she'd say was—No, she was getting married.

She was like that all the time till the wedding; George Higginson told her to drop all this schooling—what was the good of it for a commercial traveller's wife?—he didn't want a scholar, he wanted a pretty kid to come back to evenings, and take out to pictures or cuddle up at home, a pretty kid to squeeze up to, to keep a chap out of mischief—and by God, she was a warm little kid now! And Mary giggled and said yes, that was right, she didn't want any more silly old school. And she made herself peach and mauve undies, and when young George came in she hid them and then let him see a corner. Oh well, they always say the nicest time in a girl's life is when she's engaged to a fellow, don't they?

So Mary Snow got married to George Higginson, and then—well then, she just seemed to melt away, to fade right out somehow. Like an ice-cream sundae on a hot afternoon. Some girls do seem to go like that after they get married. But I've never known it to happen to anyone like it did to her. Sudden-like. "That poor little Mrs. Higginson," I said to my boy only last Sunday, "she just seems to have melted away. There's no other word for it." Once again the Snow Maiden, daughter of January and April, was hated by the sun-god, the man-god, the god of life and potency. Once again he caught her and touched her with his rays, and once again the Snow Maiden melted away, was dissolved into nothing, became no more than a story which is ended.

HANSEL AND GRETEL

Once upon a time there was a boy and a girl called Billy and Minnie Jones, and they lived in Birmingham, just like you and me. Billy was a big, lumpy, grinning boy, not quite ten, and his sister Minnie was a bit more than a year younger; because she was little and pretty and merry, she was mostly called Minnie Mouse. Their father was a mechanic, but he had been out of work for the best part of two years and had dropped out of his Union and out of the brass band he used to play in—it made him feel uncomfortable meeting the other chaps now he'd only got the one suit for Sundays and weekdays and he got to think everyone was staring at him at the band practise, so he stopped going. But he and another fellow had a bit of an allotment between them, and he spent a good lot of time down there. All the same, Mrs. Jones used to say he got that hungry after working that it wasn't worth it for the amount of vegetables he brought home.

Mrs. Jones was fed up. She couldn't help it. She'd had to make do all her life and it didn't seem somehow as if any of it had been worth living, especially the last six or seven years. She was a bit short-sighted too, but they couldn't afford glasses for her. So she was mostly cross to Billy and Minnie and they were frightened of her. Their father was nicer to them, especially when he'd made a bit, betting. He used to have a threepenny double most weeks, and sometimes it came off. Those days he used to bring back a penn'orth of mixed drops for the two children, and tell them stories; he told them fairy stories, like I'm telling you. They used to sit on his knee, smelling his breath all beery like it was every time when he'd won, and suck their sweets, and listen to the stories. But mostly Mrs. Jones was crosser than ever those days.

One afternoon she went over to the shop at the corner to get some rice and dried beans on tick, and she left Billy and Minnie at home. She told Minnie to peel the potatoes and mind she peeled them thin, and she told Billy to get on with scrubbing the kitchen floor and mind he didn't use up the soap. And then she put on her coat which was one she'd got at the Church Jumble three years back, and used to belong to the vicar's mother, who was shorter and fatter than Mrs. Jones was, but somehow, what with Mr. Jones and the children, she'd never had time to alter it, and then she went out.

After a bit Billy looked up from the floor where he was kneeling to scrub on an old wad of newspapers, and he said: "Me knees is wet. Mum won't be back, not for hours. I don't like scrubbing, Min.'" "We've got to help Mum, ain't we?" said Minnie, going on with the potatoes, "or the P.A.C. man'll catch us." "Our Min, always going on about helping Mum!" said Billy. "Proper little angel, ain't you?" Minnie threw a potato at him and he jumped up and threw the wad of newspapers from the floor at her, and she squealed because it was all squashy and cold. Then the two of them fought, oh real wicked!—and they broke one of the knobs off the fender, though goodness knows how they did it, but there, us mothers know what real tigers a pair of kids can be!

Well after that they rolled about on the floor, scrapping and biting and tearing each other's clothes, and then Minnie bumped her head on the table leg and began crying. Then Billy got sorry and gave her his dead frog that he'd got tied onto the end of a string and stuffed into his pocket—the nasty little thing—but there, you know what boys are—and they got playing with the dead frog, and Billy left off his scrubbing in the middle, and Minnie hadn't got half the potatoes done, and they were as happy as could be. And then all of a sudden Mrs. Jones came back from the shop.

She wasn't half wild with them when she saw the mess they'd got the place into, and how the floor wasn't near washed nor the potatoes near peeled, and she lammed into young Billy. He ducked under the table and she hit out, and she broke the milk jug. Now, the milk was what she'd been saving for the kids' supper—she'd done without it in her own tea for weeks now except on Sundays when she had a drop of condensed—and the jug was one she'd had for a wedding present and it belonged, as you might say, to the times when she'd thought life was worth living. And there it was all to bits on the floor, and a nasty mess to pick up, and those two kids were laughing as if it was all a joke, for breaking things mostly is a joke, to kids. So Mrs. Jones caught Billy by the collar and gave him a good smack on the face that set him off blubbering, and she shook Minnie till she'd shaken all the laughing out of her, and she called them names which I shan't repeat and which she was sorry for five minutes after, and she opened the front door and she shoved them both outside, telling them she couldn't bear the sight of them one minute longer, and she slammed it on them so that the wall shook and a bit of plaster came down off the corner, and that was another mess on the kitchen floor. And no more she could bear the sight of them just then, what with all she'd had to put up with, and seeing the groceries in the Co-op that she couldn't afford to buy for them, and having her jug broken. She didn't even try to clean it up; she just sat down by the table and let herself go slummocking all across it, and she cried and cried.

But Billy and Minnie, after the first minute or two, they didn't care. It all went off them like water off a duck's back. And off they went trotting and chattering, and along by the tram lines and under the railway arch, and past the sweet shop and past the fire station, and round the corner by the Red Lion where they hoped they might see their Dad, but they didn't, and past Mr. Butler the Pawnbroker's, which was a place they both knew pretty well, Friday evenings and Mondays, and past the chapel with the board outside about the Wrath to Come, and through the passage way and up, and so into Corporation Street itself. And there were all the gentlemen with white collars and shiny shoes and hats like the Prince of Wales, and all the ladies with real silk stockings and paint and powder on their faces, and the grand blue-chinned policemen to look after the ladies and gentlemen and make their big glossy motor-cars slide carefully along between the traffic signals this way and that. And Billy and Minnie watched the ladies and gentlemen going into the beautiful great shops and movie palaces that were just beginning to light up, all gay and golden, or with red and blue and green lights in tubes like toothpaste. And they stuck their noses and dabbed their grubby fingers against the glass, and stared and pointed at the insides of the shops, that looked so warm and cosy and full of softness and brightness and safety.

But they weren't safe really, those shops. They weren't what they looked like. Things aren't, mostly. Because, after Billy and

Minnie had been standing there for ten minutes or a quarter of an hour, who should come up to them but an old witch?

Of course, they didn't know she was a witch. And perhaps you or I wouldn't have known either. She was rather old, and she wore silk and a fur coat, very soft and warm, with another kind of fur for its collar, and she wore jewels on her ears and fingers and throat, though one didn't see them at first, because she wore gloves and kept the fur collar high over her neck, and she wore a hat with a bird's feather as bright and lovely as a fairy in it, and she stepped down carefully and circumspectly onto the pavement out of her Rolls-Royce. And she came up behind Billy and Minnie and smiled at them and said: "Now, my little dears, come along with me into the shop and I will buy you each a lovely present."

Both the children were a little bit frightened, but not frightened enough, so they went into the shop with the old witch, and they didn't dare to say a word to one another. It was all grand and huge and quiet, higher and more shining than the new Woolworth's, and full of things so beautiful and clean and new, that they could hardly breathe. They just didn't know what to choose. There were all sorts of toys and dolls and trains and teddy bears, more and bigger than they'd ever dreamt of, and they just gaped and the old witch watched them. At last Minnie suddenly made up her mind and chose a work-basket for her mother. It was ever such a beautiful work-basket, full of scissors and needles and every kind of thing, and a tape measure looking like a tiny apple and the thimble in real silver. You see, Minnie was sorry about the milk jug now, and she thought this would make up for it, and besides it would pawn for five shillings easy. But Billy was slow in making up his mind, and a bit dazed and stupid, and at last he chose a train and rails, and it was done up in a box, and then he knew he'd really have liked a meccano set or a model sports car, only it was too late.

After that, the old witch bought them each a huge box of chocolates, pink ribbon for Minnie, blue ribbon for Billy, and they tucked in, and she watched them. And then all three of them got into the Rolls-Royce and it drove off, going so softly they couldn't have told they were moving. They sat one on each side of her, rolled up in a big rug, and every now and then she smiled and glanced and shifted a little, and you could just see the tip of her tongue showing between her lips, which were rather too pink and moist-looking for anyone her age. So they drove along through the lighted, crowded streets, and the policemen held up the traffic for them and the fur rug snuggled them down into the deep cushiony seat of the car.

And Minnie thought: "Serves Mum right if we *are* late—but she won't mind really, not when she sees this." And she held tight onto her lovely, knobbly parcel, and her tongue kept on licking little bits of chocolate and stuff out from between her teeth, but she knew the box wasn't half finished yet. There was only one thing that seemed a bit funny, and that was the kind of nasty green light that there was all round the chauffeur's cap and shoulders; you could see the shape of his ears against it, and somehow she didn't think they were at all a nice shape. As it grew darker she could see this light clearer and clearer, but she couldn't say anything to Billy, because he was sitting in the other corner of the seat, with the old witch between her and him.

And then she heard a whispering and rustling at her ear, and she looked round quietly, and who should she see but the little animal which made the collar of the beautiful fur coat, watching her out of its bright, golden-dusky eyes and twitching its pretty sensitive whiskers. "You're Minnie Mouse, aren't you?" said the little animal, and she saw the white of its pointed teeth show against the soft dark of its fur.

"Yes," said Minnie, "but who ever are you?"

"I'm Sasha Sable," said the little thing, "and I'm here to warn you."

Minnie looked quickly up at the old lady's face. She was half turned away, towards Billy, and not noticing, and quite suddenly, and in spite of the work-basket and the chocolates, Minnie didn't like her at all. "What of?" whispered Minnie; "her?"

"Yes," said Sasha Sable, "she's a horrible witch. She had me killed to make into the collar of her coat. I was caught by the foot in one of her traps while I and my friends were jumping and dancing along over the snow. My friends ran away from the smell of iron and my blood and I was there three days trying to get out of the trap, and all the time the trap was crushing my foot and the cold was biting at my wound. I tried to gnaw my foot off to get out of her trap, Minnie, but I couldn't; I stayed there squealing or dead-quiet till the fourth day, and then one of her slaves came and killed me, and skinned my fur off my poor body. But to-day I have been allowed to come alive and warn you against my mistress the witch."

Minnie put up her hand softly and stroked the soft paw of Sasha Sable that had been crushed in the trap and whispered to him to go on.

"It was the same for the other animals in her coat," said Sasha Sable, "we were all made to suffer pain and death for her. And the fairy bird in her hat, he was snared between one flower and another, and his neck wrung. Do you know about the silk she's wearing, Minnie Mouse? There were little children out in China, and she trapped them like she trapped the rest of us, and every day they had to dip their hands into boiling water to fetch out the cocoons of the dead silk-worms to be spun into her dresses."

"What ever happened to the children in the end?" said Minnie, going all shivery.

"They died, mostly. That's what witches do with children. They kill them and eat them and turn them into spiders or bake them into gingerbread. She's got slaves all over the world. She's got brown slaves who dive into the sea to pull Jane Oyster out of her bed and cut her open to steal her pearls, and sometimes they get caught by the great clams and octopuses and drowned; she's got black slaves who work in the hot diamond pits for her. And here too, she has her slaves at work the whole time, making things for her and carrying them to her house. The P.A.C. man is one of her slaves, Minnie; he's got to do it because she makes him. And now I've warned you so you'd better get away before she gets you too."

"But—" said Minnie. Only just then the old witch turned her head and as she did so Sasha Sable flattened out, and his eyes were only beads and his paws went limp and dangled, and he was just the collar of the fur coat. The witch smiled at Minnie, but Minnie ducked her head over the parcel; she couldn't smile back. She was thinking of the fairy tales her Dad used to tell her on lucky nights, and what the witches in the fairy tales used to do to children. She remembered knives and cauldrons and fires waiting, and how the children in the stories were fattened up to be eaten, and she wished she'd thought of that before starting to eat the chocolates, and she felt a bit sick.

Now the Rolls-Royce was sliding along a wide road, with big houses on each side, set far apart from one another in gardens, and by and bye they turned into a drive and the headlights of the car lighted up thick, spiky looking, dangerous bushes which parted in front of them, and they came to the stone steps and the wide front door of the witch's house. It was quite dark by now, but the headlights of the Rolls-Royce shining along the house showed Minnie that it was built of solid gold and silver, only both beautiful metals had been tarnished and dirtied over by the smoke of the Midlands, and ivy had been trained up the golden pillars to make them look more respectable. A butler in a black coat opened the great front door and the old witch walked in; and behind her came Billy and Minnie, hand in hand. Minnie hadn't yet had time to explain to Billy what Sasha Sable had told her, and he wanted to go in; he thought there would be more trains and chocolates and meccano sets. Inside, the gold and silver house was papered with pound notes and ten shilling notes, and the drawing-room with crossed cheques for a thousand pounds apiece. The kitchen and pantry were papered in stripes with sheets of stamps, and the passages with postal orders; the lamp-shades were made of Bank of England five-pound notes, and the thick rustling carpets of dollars and francs and marks and lire and pesetas and yen and I don't know what-all else. All that was the magic the old witch used when she wanted to bewitch people and kill them or enslave them or turn them into lizards and spiders and toads.

Suddenly Billy said: "I want to go home. Oo, I do want to go home to Dad and Mum!" But the old witch said: "Not to-night, my dear, too late for little boys to go out now. To-morrow perhaps." And Minnie pinched him to stop him answering back, for she was afraid that if he did they would both get snapped up at once. Then the butler in the black coat took them into a room where they found a lovely supper of cake and milk and fruit, and Billy began to gobble it up, but Minnie didn't want to. They tried to talk to the butler, but it was no good; the witch had made him dumb with her enchantments.

At last he went away and then Minnie whispered to Billy just what Sasha Sable had told her. "Oh Min, whatever shall we do?" said Billy, and he began to cry, but Minnie had more sense than that. So when he stopped crying, they peeped out of the room and went creeping about the house, trying to find a way out. But all the doors and windows were fastened up by great heavy golden bars, that they couldn't begin to lift, and once or twice when they looked quietly round a corner, there'd be someone standing with his back to them at the end of a corridor, and he'd have that nasty green light round his head and shoulders, the same as the chauffeur had.

Once they came into the room where the old witch was sitting, playing Patience beside a nice warm fire. But when they looked, they saw that it wasn't good Derby brights on the fire, but a heap of blackened bones that the pretty flames were dancing about among. And they saw it wasn't a pussy-cat on the hearth-rug, but a small tiger that was watching them. And they saw she wasn't playing Patience with ordinary cards, because the clubs were factories and rows of little houses, and the spades were acres of land, and the diamonds were stocks and shares, and the hearts were people's lives, so whenever she discarded a heart it bled a little, and the blood dripped off the table, down its jade and ivory legs, and the cat that was really a tiger, only worse, lapped up the blood. And the witch looked up from her Patience and patted their heads, and seemed very satisfied, and then she told them to run along to bed.

So the dumb butler in the black coat took them to another beautiful room where there were two little beds with knobs of rubies and emeralds, and two little suits of pyjamas with a £ sign embroidered on the pocket. Neither of them had ever had a bed like that; it reminded Minnie of the week she'd been in hospital with her bad leg, only it was even grander, and the sheets whiter, and the blankets softer. So they got into the pyjamas, which were like what they'd seen in shop windows, and danced about in them a bit, only the embroidery on the pocket seemed to burn rather and gave them a pain over the heart. So they got into bed, but they were afraid to talk to one another, because they thought that the emerald and ruby knobs might be listening.

The next thing that happened was that they heard steps outside and in came the old witch to tuck them up and say good-night. She kissed Billy who was just lying staring at her, but Minnie was pretending to be asleep and had burrowed her face down under the blanket, so the witch couldn't get at her. When she went out, she put out all the lights, except for a little lamp that was made to look like a lighthouse, and on the very top of it was an old-fashioned golden sovereign, like I remember when I was a kid myself years and years ago, but you don't. And the horrid thing was that every now and then a pretty pale moth would come fluttering up and bang against the light, and burn its wings. Not that moths don't do that anywhere where there's a light, let alone in witches' houses, but somehow there were more moths in that room than there'd any right to be in a city like Birmingham. And hearing the moth's wings sizzle and the soft plopping down of their silly little bodies as they fell and died, was more than Minnie could stand. She'd been wondering hard how to do in the witch, remembering the way the children in the fairy tales used to manage it, tipping her up into her own oven and turning her into gingerbread—only there didn't seem to be any oven here and she didn't know what else would do. So now, what with lying awake, and watching the nasty little lighthouse lamp and the glitter on the ruby and emerald knobs, and hearing the sizzle and drop of the burnt moths, one after the other, she began to call in a whisper for Sasha Sable to come and help her. But as to Billy, after the witch had kissed him he went to sleep and began to dream about more and better trains and model aeroplanes and parlour-games and baby cinema sets and small-scale jazz bands and all the other things that the witch had put into his head with her enchantments.

So now it was only Minnie Mouse who lay awake, biting her fingers and whispering for Sasha Sable and feeling the £ mark on her pyjama pocket burning and biting her. She was, as you might say, all alone, for that snoring little Billy wasn't any comfort. And first it struck the half hour and then it struck the hour, and then there came a pattering and rustling of little furry feet, and all of a sudden the lighthouse went out and the ruby and emerald knobs stopped glittering, and Minnie knew that Sasha Sable had come alive again.

"Minnie Mouse, Minnie Mouse!" said the little dusky beast, "did you let her kiss you?"

"No!" said Minnie. "Oh, where are you?" And she reached out in the dark till her fingers fell on and fondled his soft warm fur.

"Then you can get away," said Sasha Sable. "You've only got to follow me and I'll show you the back door that they always forget to bolt."

Minnie jumped out of bed; she was beginning to be able to see in the dark. She pulled off the pyjamas and got back as quick as she could into her old patched vest and her serge knickers and frock, and her socks that were more holes and darns than anything else, and her old black shoes that had come from the Church Jumble, the same as her mother's coat and about as bad a fit—but she didn't mind that now. Then she began to shake her brother. "Billy!" she said, "Wake up, can't you! Oh Billy, wake up!"

But it was no good. Billy slept like a log, and when she bent right over close to him she could see he was smiling in a silly sort of way. Sasha Sable jumped onto the bed. "There's only one thing to be done," he said, "or else we'll never wake him." And he bit Billy's finger with his sharp white teeth and then stuffed his tail into Billy's mouth to stop him making a noise crying. But that woke Billy up all right, though at first he didn't like being woke, for he'd been in the middle of dreaming that he'd got a bicycle and was riding it up and down an enormous shop full of toys and games, choosing things as he went along. Still, after he'd rubbed his eyes for a minute or two he began to see sense, and Minnie pulled off his pyjama jacket and helped him into his things. "Come along," said Sasha Sable.

Minnie was just coming when she stumbled over her parcel. "Oh!" she said, "can I take my work-basket?"

Sasha Sable made a grumbling noise between his teeth. At last he said: "Very well. But mind, you can't take the chocolates, Minnie Mouse, and that silly brother of yours can't take his parcel; it's too big." And he looked round over his shoulder and said: "If you whine, Billy, I'll bite you again. So there."

Then Minnie opened the door of the room and they all three went out. Sasha Sable trotted in front of them down the passage, which was still lighted up, though there was no one about. Seeing him like that, so small and pretty and unafraid, made Minnie stop being frightened too. She bent down and whispered to him: "Can't Billy and me kill the old witch? The kids in the fairy tales always do."

"Not yet," said Sasha Sable, cocking up his muzzle and bright eyes at her. "Next time, perhaps. If you're a good girl and remember all about it and never let the witch get at you again." And then he added: "You might as well take one of those lamp-shades away with you. Your Dad and Mum'll thank you, and perhaps it'll help you to remember."

So Minnie and Billy stripped off the Bank of England notes that made the lamp-shade and put them into their pockets, and then they followed Sasha Sable down some steps and round a corner and so to a little door that seemed to be made of ordinary wood instead of gold or silver. They opened it quite easily. "Good-bye, Sasha Sable," said Minnie, and held out her arms.

He jumped into them and nestled all soft against her neck and chin for a minute. "Good-bye, Minnie Mouse," he said, "I must go back or she'll miss me from the collar of her grand coat. But remember, when the time comes, if you want help in the witch's house, there'll always be me—or someone else." And then he jumped down and scuttled off into the house, and they shut the door carefully after him.

They ran down the path and through the shrubbery; the spiky nasty evergreens tried to catch at them, but all they did was to tear a hole in Billy's coat, and then they were out in the road and standing under an ordinary street-lamp, and very sleepy. Billy's finger was still bleeding where Sasha Sable had bitten him, and neither of them had a hanky to tie it up, but he sucked it and said he was all right, and was a bit nice to Minnie, because now she was tired and crying a little and saying she'd never get home.

Still, they did get home all right, and not more than an hour later, for when they got down onto the main road again, what should they do but get a lift from a lorry that was going their way. Whether Sasha Sable had anything to do with that, I don't know. Most likely he hadn't; a lorry driver'll always give you a lift if you ask him nicely and he isn't being speeded up so that he daren't stop—and his boss isn't looking. When he put them down they'd only a quarter of an hour's walk home, but all the same Mr. and Mrs. Jones were in an awful state when they got back. They'd been round to the police and the hospital and everything and both of them burst out crying and hugging them, especially Mrs. Jones, she felt that bad about having turned them out earlier on. She was as pleased as pie when Minnie gave her the work-basket, and then the kids remembered about the lamp-shade and turned out their pockets, and sure enough, there were the Bank-notes, fivers and tenners, so that Mr. and Mrs. Jones couldn't hardly believe their eyes.

Then Billy and Minnie tried to explain all about their adventures, but no one believed them, no more than you do, I'll be bound. But all the same the Bank-notes were good enough. Only Mr. Jones, being a sensible man and not wanting it to get round to the P.A.C. man, took them over to his cousin who was an upholsterer in Walsall and he changed them for him, only taking a shilling in the pound which wasn't too bad. And Mrs. Jones paid up all her bills, and they both began to hold up their heads again with the neighbours, and altogether things took a turn for the better, as you might say. It ended with Mr. Jones moving over to Walsall and getting a job in the upholstery line with his cousin. Only he missed the allotment.

But how Billy and Minnie grew up, and how later on they went back to the witch's house, and how they and their friends killed the old witch—for she was still going strong—and made things so that she could never come back again to Birmingham or anywhere else, that's another story and I haven't time to tell it you to-day.

BIRMINGHAM AND THE ALLIES

The Chinese fairies go by with a wavering graciousness
Curtseying to those who pass the State examinations.
Behind them the hoho birds droop from the classic rockeries,
Filling the proud minds of the wild poets with bursts of plumes,
Mozart liked wild strawberries with white wine in withy
    arbours,
Handel liked sprigged muslin with high heels. There exist also
Certain occurrences in the present, certain dispositions and
    persons:
Things common and well known and not difficult,
The boys listening to the music, the rain drops on the
    wind-screen,
New bread at evening, the Pole Star over Stirchley,
Tom Baxter, Walter Priest, Claud Ames and Harold Nash,
Sid Hines, Len Edwards, Ted Simmons, Leon Thompson, May
    Cooke.

The Chinese fairies respect learning, but have compassion on
    ignorance;
The minds of the fierce poets are set on a fresh mood;
European democracy in sprigged muslin is taking tea with
    Handel;
The boys are looking at the Pole Star, the tension is broken by
    the rain.

But there exists also Power,
And flags and cruelty and an increasing profit on evil,
The men with the large cheque-books and their laughing and ig-
    norant women.
Handel and Mozart did not write music suitable for
    cheque-books,
Suitable for leaders in lime-light, suitable for stirring the
    passions
Of hate and cruelty.
They are no good to the men with the money. Nor are
Learning and compassion and poetry or the remote Pole Star.
    Nor yet
Democracy..
Nor yet Tom Baxter, Sid Hines, May and Alf Cooke, Claud
    Ames,
Harold, Ted, Len, Ethel, Jo and Jack.
You have been defeated once, and the next time
Less will be left you. And the hoho birds have been snared
To make hat plumage for the rich and ignorant women.

Between one nightmare and the next nightmare
We turn in our sleep, make certain dispositions:
It would be well to have definite contacts, there or here,
It would be well to consult the allies, to discuss tactics,
Before darkness falls again and the driving of the blind
    nightmares.
It is even possible that we might wake and find
We had made ourselves a day.

Breaking the nightmare with a great effort we may yet discover
The learned and compassionate fairies going by at daybreak,
We with the boys hearing the music, eating the new bread,
The dawn rain-fresh over Stirchley, and our friends with us
    waking.
We may discover we have been wise and wary,
Twisting defeat
Into a net for the men who snared the fairies.
We may have snared ourselves power.
And in the snaring changed it.

(King's Norton—Abbotsholme. Nov. 1935.)

SORIA MORIA CASTLE

(for G.D.H.C.)

About sunset, a castle had been constructed upon the sands; I had, in fact, a good deal to do with it myself. Shortly afterwards I had passed over the cardboard drawbridge and under the silver-paper portcullis, nor was it until the feathery and tinkling clang of the latter, falling into place with the utmost finality behind me, had aroused my hitherto bemused senses, that I began to ask myself whether, after all, I had been wise in the decision which it seemed certain I had but lately come to. It was by then, however, too late, and on the first bend of that sharp upward zigzag, cut, as I well remembered, with the larger blade of an old penknife, that I encountered the witch, with her skirts spread round her and her head bent over a half-knitted stocking of that curious dark murrey colour, as far removed from true purple as it is from clear red, which is the preferred underwear tint of all Unlikely Persons. She begged me to excuse her until she had finished the row of knitting, which, indeed, I was glad enough to do, since it gave me an excuse for considering my position, not of course that such consideration had any practical value at this juncture of affairs.

She then conducted me up the various flights of the zigzag, talking in such a manner that I could never be certain whether it would be more tactful of me to join in or not to appear to be listening. There would certainly have been a fine view from the upper flights of the zigzag, had the refocussing of my vision, consequent upon the alteration of my scale of material standards, allowed of it; I must confess, also, that it became increasingly unpleasant to consider how much nearer, with each flight of the zigzag, we were approaching the mouth of the square entrance of the castle. The witch appeared to have guessed what I had in mind, for she turned to me and said in a most aggrieved voice: "If you hadn't decided to come to Soria Moria castle, you didn't need to have gone and built it!"

"But," I said, "there were reasons against the Castle East of the Sun." And I remembered for a moment with extreme distinctness the committee meeting in which we had all so tediously, and as I thought at the time, so needlessly, discussed the necessity for realism.

"Reasons!" she said, "you didn't think you were fit to be trusted with reasons, did you?" And she snorted at me, and tucked the knitting under one arm.

"No," I said. "In a way that is so. But there were others."

"More fools they," said the witch; "as if they didn't know I can't get through more than one of you in a month, these days, what with my new false teeth and the times being what they are! Get along in with you!" And she suddenly and unexpectedly gave me the most unpleasant shove into the dark entrance of Soria Moria castle.

The facts as they appeared were quite incontrovertible and more displeasing than I can well express. The cauldron was hooked over a small fire on my left. It was quite beyond my power to look at what it contained or indeed to take any kind of direct glance at it, but the smell which arose from it was of so discouraging a nature that I began to find it very hard to stand upright, nor was the very business-like triangular knife lying on the kitchen table any less unreassuring. For, although it seems for the first minute or two quite unthinkable that such things should be in any way connected with oneself, yet there was no possible way of escaping the conclusion that they were. It was only at this point that it began to dawn on me what kind of reality the committee had so guardedly referred to towards the end of our discussion, and as I observed the back of the witch ferreting about in her kitchen cupboard for certain herbs and accompaniments, I became filled with extreme indignation at the fact that reality was so astonishingly different at close quarters. Fortunately, this indignation was accompanied by the customary outpouring of secretion from the adrenal glands which, in their turn, re-affected the muscles and sinews of my back and legs to such a degree that I now resolved to accept nothing without the fiercest possible struggle.

As the witch turned round I said to her, "I am not going into your cauldron!" She did not answer but proceeded to look at me in a curiously fixed and horrible way, as though she were seeing me, my own highly important and cossetted self, as so many pounds of meat. At the same time saliva dripped from her lower lip and from what I could not help recollecting were her new false teeth. This look almost succeeded in reducing me to my former condition of complete discouragement, and had I not made a sudden move, it would certainly have done so. However, I snatched up the triangular knife from the table and threatened her with it. The witch's look immediately lost some of its disgusting impersonality, and she made a sign with two fingers at the knife, which promptly lighted at the tip and, being apparently made of magnesium or some similar metal or alloy, flared up blindingly as I dropped it between myself and the cauldron, and threw one hand up over my eyes. When I could see again, the witch's back was towards me once more, and she was muttering to herself. When she turned she had three small objects in her hand. "Well, if you won't go into the cauldron," she said, and her voice broke off into mutters of "Most annoying, most annoying," and she held out her hand towards me: "You may choose whichever you like."

"I don't see why I should!" I said, almost crying with anger and misery at the idea of being compelled to touch and accept any one of these three ambiguous little objects. At the same time, however, I did see, only too clearly, that there was no possibility of evasion, nor, for that matter, of prolonging the affair indefinitely by any argument. The light in the cave was none of the best, especially as the entrance had, as might have been expected, crumbled inwards immediately after the vibration of our tread had unsettled the sand particles of which it was, after all, composed. There was no telling where any one of the three choices would carry me. I chose at random the middle one of the three objects, which was no other than a grain of common wheat.

Immediately three sensations overwhelmed me: a sensation of shrinking, a sensation of hardening and a sensation of darkening. They were not in any way painful and yet they concealed a profound tension, as though from shrinking and hardening I must needs burst forth into sudden softness, and as though my present darkness must collapse into a starred rent. So for a time I waited, with no sense of place in any world or passage of any measurable period of days or months. Only the tension slowly increased until it became apparent that the constriction was about to yield to some violent and now localised pressure. My whole self was become intent on a growing point, and soon enough the constriction and darkness which had been part of me for so long were parted, and I knew my white and tender root had begun to feel downwards through a different darkness and a hardness unexpectedly creviced for the forcing of ways; soon afterwards, too, my upper growing point had begun its struggle through fissures in a yielding hardness with an extension of special feeling to the phototropic cell-cluster now hourly expecting the dazzle of reward. I had by this almost forgotten the hardness and tension of the safe grain life, but my rapidly separating growing-points were a-tingle with ever-present danger. What horrors of drought or rotting wetness, above all of blind, remorseless, chewing mouths! And yet my growth was momently attaining a toughness which could outface all.

And now the upper shoot had pierced into a gratification of warm light; the cell layers spread and flattened to receive gifts. Green grains of chlorophyll had appeared in my upper layers, immediately specialising my vaguely rampant growth into the delightful pattern of a sun-needing plant; while below my pale busy fibres sucked up a constant stream of success from the dark earth which anchored me. As I grew I began to be aware that I was not alone. With the drawing-out of sun and rain my green leaves overlapped the leaves of my neighbours, catching from them a delicate tingle of response. Nor, in the warm days and cool nights of early summer could any of the wheatfield have been less than utterly satisfied with the tender and neighbourly response of stem to stem, the effortless rippling and stretching as the breezes tossed us, the effortless breathing in and out in our daily and nightly rhythm, our age-old vegetable ordering of the gaseous elements that gently blanket the ever-living world. Effortless too, the stooping under warm rain that slithered down our stems to our matted and neighbourly rootlets. Effortless, the shaking off of the shining drops; effortless our constant growth, supported and supporting, one by the other. And by now each was aware, in its own midst, and in the midst of its neighbours in the uncounted community of the harvest field, of that for which all was a preparation. Tenderest leaflets now unfolded from our green grain spikes, plumed with the delicate pale grass flowers, stigmas as yet half uncoiling and unaware, stamens with the light gold burden of half ripe pollen grains.

There came then a day, indeed a succession of days, when the long pouring down of warmth had aroused us all to the same quivering pitch of waiting inaction about to be loosed at a last climax of ripeness. And then, with a parting and shedding and minute splitting of cell walls, there was cast wide upon the calm warm air about our upflung soft seed-spikes such a multitude of floating pollen grains that the very nature of our environment became changed. The light rays from the sun became paths for these scarce-weighted particles which, as though they had been only molecules of matter, could be deflected and driven by the low battering of light. Thus, then, our stigmas received them in open certainty of righteousness. Neighbour to neighbour, our unity was now in this mixing completed; we of the wheatfield having given out were now receiving, as the pollen cells nested on the open slopes of the stigmas poured themselves out in hastening long tongues of transparent life towards the awaiting seed cell, which, when at last a pollen tongue laid hold of it, became what it was meant to be, settling with a new toughness into the common life of the corn.

How, then, put into words, the days following? For by the middle of summer we were all part of one life, through our fertility losing our identity, but ever in a daze of dancing leaves and hardening stems through which now juices scarcely crept, a daze of the mingling and splitting of cells, a uniting and casting off of chromosomes, each one a single wheat plant and yet each inseparably and inextricably part of the others. And now in our joint consciousness we became aware of a new need, since the earth no longer anchored us securely and yet our heaviness was between us and the wind. No longer did we feel identity with those roots which had been our earliest and most passionate point of intenseness. Our stems and leaves had almost lost hold on life; we had become concentrated upon the heavy goldenness of our bowing heads.

There was no pain as the steel blade severed our stems, no shock of parting from earth. Our golden heads lay ever thicker and more neighbourly in harvest. There was no pain in the threshing; all growth was dormant, and without growth there is no pain. Nor did the seed corn which was made separate from the bread corn rejoice or grieve in any way at its destiny. There was no pain in the grinding, but only wonder, and a still more profound mixing of essences.

For some indefinite time we lay slackly as flour, sacked or binned, in dusk and formless. Then hands were laid on us and there was a new mixing, with substances which were at first alien and then became part of us, bringing with them faint, diffuse memories of a hotter sun and different growth, or of an animal life, incomprehensible and yet acceptable. Thus, by the time of the baking, all the ingredients had mingled in intimate combination of starch, sugar, milk-fat and protein molecules, making a smooth and homogeneous substance, which at last, cake-shaped and oven-hot, gathered itself into a single consciousness, so that again there was an "I," individual and yet in a complete sympathy with the other cakes which had been formed out of the same material. I then, as a cake-individual, was proudly and gaily decorated with a cake's final and not least fripperies of coloured icing, split cherries and green pistachio nuts, which, expertly laid upon me, became part of my rich and copious edibility. I was now carefully placed upon paper and that again on a platter, and so, by mid-morning, though whether of summer or winter I cannot tell, onto a shelf behind a great shining sheet of glass interposing itself completely between my white and pink immobility and the jostling and dusty street.

Beside me on the shelf were other cakes, my sisters, they too all a-glisten with pinks and blues and shimmering bridal white, and I was aware that they too were all rounded towards fulfilment of themselves. They too were longing for the appraising eye, forerunner of the more appraising lips and tongue; they too knew themselves made for the sale, the handing-over, the ritual wrapping and unwrapping, the setting upon a strange table, the knife and the laying-open, above all the sacred and basic awakening and satisfying of hunger. We were aware now that beyond the great screen of glass, eyes were looking at us, the living eyes of hunger and delicious greed: oh if we could but have given ourselves at once to its satisfying, now with our hearts still warm from the oven, and our icing snow-cool and fresh, unhardened by time and the tarnishing caress of air! Thus would we, without wearying and in our first freshness, have become one with life. And occasionally, indeed, one of us might be taken up and sold and given to the eyes and the final assuagement of hunger. Yet this was rare, and as the day passed and the last oven-warmth died out of the midst of each of us, our impatience grew and lay heavy upon us. Lights were switched on above us in the shop and a richer glow came on the smooth sugar, and the eyes of hunger and greed trailed past us, and now and then a finger was dabbed upon the plate glass. Yet by the evening few of us had taken on their fulfilment. We passed the night in darkness, still in the shop.

The next morning again we were set out, again we offered our sweetness and richness to the eyes behind the glass. But by now it was becoming apparent to me that those eyes in which pure, sharp hunger itself was the dominating force—eyes whose live bodies we on the cake shelves most longed to satisfy—were not the same eyes as those of our purchasers, which were in general illumined by a less frank and to us desirable force. For it seemed to us that among these purchasers, most of whom were women, elaborate as ourselves in pinks and blues and silks that shone almost like icing, there were those who might merely and brutally use a cake—a cake made for the food of mankind—for the decoration of a party; there were those, it seemed to us, who might languidly and without appetite shear off a thin slice and unadmiringly consume or perhaps only crumble it, leaving the great body of the cake to wither and dry up and at last be eaten grudgingly and ingloriously; there were those, we thought, who would not scruple to throw away a half-eaten cake into hideous non-fulfilment. But why then, why could the hungry eyes not choose out and buy the cake they needed and which needed them? We did not know, we only wanted to be a satisfaction instead of a temptation to the hungry eyes.

So passed a second day and a third, and a strange weariness and heaviness began to come on me and such of my sisters as still shared my loneliness. We felt that we were no longer so delicious, so assuaging as we had been. Our sugar icing had hardened un-kindly, here a cherry was loose upon us, there a nut. And still the many hungry and the few who could buy! It was after the lights were turned on that this pressure of eyes upon us became almost more than we could bear. We knew obscurely that some of these eyes belonged to children finished with school, children who would seize on us joyously and unashamedly with both hands, gobbling us whole-heartedly into their growing life. And others belonged to men coming back from labour, hard work of hands and bodies which had left their muscles worn and fainting for sugar to burn up and reconstitute them; we knew the great hun-gry mouths of these men and the teeth that would meet on us and the strength we would become in them. And yet other eyes belonged to women whose thoughts, beating upon us through the unmoved glass, were of many hungers, their own and their husbands' and their children's, and we knew that if one of these women could have had us on her table, there would have been no crumb left unpraised and uneaten. But those hungry eyes passed and hesitated and passed reluctantly on, in an endless stream, and none might cross the threshold and take us from the shop into their homes.

And so passed days, and with them a terrible discouragement to the cakes which no one had bought, which had lost their freshness, which had hardened and dried and cracked a little. And the cakes knew the fear of mildew and crumbling and of being no longer fit for the assuagement and life-making of mankind. And the sugar on the cakes was a little flecked with dust, and pieces had broken off here and there; they were handled roughly morning and evening. And it came about that one morning the master of the shop bade his servants to clear out the old rubbish, and I and the other cakes which had not been sold were bundled together, breaking as they did so. A piece here and there was picked up and eaten by the servants of the baker, but mostly the stuff of the cakes had become dry and unpalatable, so that even the eyes of the very hungry would not have looked on them with any pleasure. And I and the other cakes were thrown out on the dust heap and it was as though we had never been of the stuff of cakes.

And with that I was again standing before the witch in Soria Moria castle, but there was yet in my body and mind a terrible dryness and fear, so that I could scarcely face her. She was sitting beside the cauldron going on with that stocking, and the smell which rose from the cauldron was no more attractive than it had been. She looked at me and sniffed and wiped her nose with the half-knitted stocking. "So you're back, are you?" she said. I nodded, being still unable to speak. "Bad pennies," she said. "Well, you'll just have to have another turn. Or of course if you didn't want to—" She licked her lips and glanced towards the cauldron, just as a small and purposeful seeming flame jetted from below it, giving me sufficient illumination for me to see that her hand was crooked into half openness. Nor did I wait for another word from her, but immediately snatched up the next of the small objects out of her palm.

The same sensations overcame me as had done so upon the first occasion, shrinking and hardness and darkness. And again the tension, becoming unbearable, broke into pale, thready growing-points, a pushing up towards light and warmth and down towards dampness and anchorage. And again I grew and spread green leaves and sucked through their pores the gases which dissolved through my warm chloroplasts. But this time I was a stronger growth, my stem thickened and became the chief part of me; strong cells within clustered and pushed and became the bud-points of branchlets. Rain and sun passed over me; my fibrous roots clung onto rock, sucking the life-giving soil salts away from weaker, brittler root-growths. In autumn my leaves fell, no longer part of me, and became food for me as they rotted; and in winter I rested, scarcely aware of my aliveness, only a core of potentials between twiggy dry stem and twiggy clinging roots. There was a man who bent over me in my winter sleep and sheared the thin end of my stem and took from round me the weeds, they too half dead. But all this passed me by, until in Spring I came alive again, with swelling and splitting of cells, rush up of sap, hurry towards the hot bright sun which drew the tendrils of the young vines after him all across and across the well-tended vineyard.

And so, for me as a vine, seasons went by, and at last I was to be part of the vintage; I put forth flowers, I sent out pollen and received it again, the minute green cell clusters swelled to berries, hard seed and around it the growing pulp that sucked up and stored the sugar out of my sap. I was aware of my neighbours then, although less closely than when I had been a wheat plant, but I knew that they too had brought forth grape bunches and were holding and feeding them in the shade of their leaves. I was aware too of the men who came, aware of their pride in me, dimly aware of their purpose with me and my grapes. I endured the pain of the summer pruning, and the shearing of the smallest bunches, knowing that the great purpose was coming closer upon us. I endured the spraying, the branding and spotting of my wild loveliness by the ugly security of the cuprous solution. My leaves bent carefully, sheltering the bunches from a too drying sun, or from rain which might spoil the bloom which now had begun to dawn wonderfully upon the baby skin of my grapes. More and more, the "I" that I was became concentrated upon the ripening grape-bunches, purpose and intention of my existence. There was now a mingled sweetness in the still air of the vineyard, breathed out from the compact proletarian bunches of good wine-grapes, so that our selves, pollinated from one another, became inextricably one by the time that the vintage was upon us.

For a time now, as at harvest, I was no self of my own, but part of an experience which was re-shaping the whole purport of our joint being. It was thus in the cutting of the grape bunches and the heavy dumping of the full berries into the baskets and the heavier, steadier pouring out of the berries into the vats against whose sides the bursting mass heaved and pressed, so that the juice began to run and flow together from the grapes of all the vines of the vineyard. There was more pressure and more bursting until there was no grape which had not broken through its tough delicate skin and poured out its stored sweetness. And then there began a strange movement, a tossing and prickling and dizzying, so that for a time this being of which I was a part was lost and transported into a sweet chaos; our crushed and spilled life had been invaded by another life, seizing upon and struggling with and dancing among our warm grape-sugar. While this went on, at first there was constant motion and interpenetration of substances, but later all was dark and quiet, the full fermentation of the wine having brought to agreement all struggle. We rested in the casks.

It was not until later that I became again a separate self, enclosed in the smoothly fitting glass of a wine bottle, wisely stoppered with cork. Yet the stopper and the bottle were both so much part of me that I could feel through them and know myself one of many, of a deep and cool cellar, breathing out flower sweetness to the unstirring air. And I knew that we all waited to be poured into the tingling throats, the hastening blood, of men and women, who through us would become braver and happier and more generous, makers of songs and stories, adventurers and lovers. This was our noble destiny; for this we had once been given the name of a God.

Thus then the embottled wine sang in the darkness of its Dionysian fate. Men and women had formed and tended us and taken thought for us; we had become aware of their needs and dreams. We had divine understanding of tiredness and discouragement, and how it was in us to allay these sadnesses. We knew the pains of those who cannot escape from the toils of their selves and their own miseries and knew too how we could help them to escape, show them the way out of self-pity and self-regard to comradeship and philosophy and kindliness. We understood that we held the secret of the crack in time, so that all those oppressed with vain endeavour and the fleet passing of life and love might through us become aware that there is also eternity. For us in darkness flashed by the leaping leopards of poetry, swept close the moth wings of rest and relaxing, bubbled the pure gaiety of youth and friendship, the springing of ideas, the springing of love and the setting free from bonds. So we waited, sure of our gifts.

I do not know how long we lay in darkness, only I know that all the time the song in us was growing stronger and sweeter; we felt ourselves better able to fulfil our destiny. And then came light, and hands on me and voices and I was aware of how soon I should know my fate, to what pains I should give healing or to what creation I should inspire. And I was taken up and carefully placed upon a table, among glasses, and there were men all round me, and I was become such that I was aware of their thoughts and feelings towards me.

And I saw first that they were not sad nor discouraged nor in travail of work or love, since they were all rich and secure and well-fed and driven by no necessities. I had no need to heal them. So it seemed to me that perhaps they were creators. But that was not so either; they were not of those who wish to give out, but only to take; there was no spark in them which I could fan to flame of adventurousness or art or love or deep thought. So then, perhaps, they must surely be good friends, laughter-loving, with their minds thrown open each to the other. But neither was that so, for in their hearts was suspicion and jealousy and quarrelsomeness; each man was the slave of himself and his own possessions, and being slaves they could not also be friends. But it seemed to me, even with this, that maybe I could break down these barriers between them and give them happiness, for, although they were not sad, they were yet not happy. And with that the stopper was taken from my bottle and I was poured into glasses, beautiful and tingling and full of hope.

But none of these men saw me as beautiful; they only saw me as a thing which had cost them money, as another piece of possession and pride. And I was swallowed and my essences entered into them, evoking response from nerve and brain cells. But vain my hopes. For the thing which they had been fashioned into by their life—the thing which they had allowed themselves to become—was not to be altered. True enough, bonds were loosened in them, but these were bonds not of uncertainty or a lonely enclosure in the self, but bonds of restraint and a certain outward decency. Such of these men as had small resentments and hatreds hidden in them, let them come out in boasting and anger; loosed too, the impulses towards cruelty. For it was my fate to set free not only the good in mankind but also the evil, not only the dreams of beauty but the nightmares of ugliness, and so, having done what I was meant to do, but having seen it turned to manifest wickedness, I was dissolved and possessed by these men, and lost forever, and out of this overwhelming loss and misery and wan hope, I found myself again facing the witch and again, as I knew, with a nonhuman destiny before me.

I did not hesitate, for the cauldron was still there in its place, and the witch nodded affably enough as she opened her hand with the third choice, which was larger than the others. As I touched it, I saw by a momentary flicker of light, that it was a small piece of iron ore.

Again there was hardness and darkness, but this time no sense of pressure. All, all was stayed. It would have been the same to have waited for a moment or for eternity, nor can I in any way guess at the duration of time that actually passed; I had no measure for it of urgency or growth or consciousness. The blasting of the iron-stone shook me but did not waken me. Inert I was mined and loaded on trucks and sent many miles by train or lorry. Only, the whole time, I was gathering to myself, not any kind of life, for I was and must remain non-living matter, but a sense which was like neither human nor plant sense, of the men who handled me. And the me that I was spread indefinitely beyond that small piece of ore which the witch had handed out, so that there was continuity between one truck-load and another.

Then came the writhing heat of furnaces and the separating of metal from slag, and at the end of that period my strange sense had followed the metal into bars of pig-iron, although, for all I knew, it might also be with the slag; but of that I could have no knowledge. Men handled the pig-iron strongly and angrily, sweating and sometimes in pain. I knew why they were angry, how they, like iron itself, were gripped by an inexorable process which they could not anyhow escape from. I sensed that they had thoughts of another life or of this work of theirs made somehow different and for different ends. They were not glad of the purpose of their life; they would have had it otherwise.

And again there were furnaces and now, instead of a separation, a mixing with another element, a toughening. Again cool, I was piled into ingots of steel in some vast warehouse and again there was in me a knowledge of the men who had thought out and worked upon their fashioning, and this knowledge was certain and unmoving and metallic, as though the shine on my surface, the different refraction of molecules, was in some way sympathetic with that brightness which comes on the thought of men and women when they consider some making which they mean to do. There were within my packed substance, an interlocking and overlapping multiplicity of images, set upon me by the ingenious imaginations of skilled designers, the latest children of the busy centuries of iron-working, begun when I was strengthless and purposeless ore, deep-hidden and utterly unaware. These interimposed three-dimensional images showed sometimes the simplest human necessities, cooking pots and spades and ploughshares, beds for loving and sleeping, tables for feasting and working; showered and danced through me like electrons the thousand shapes of little things, needles and knives and buttons and razor blades, the pin for the baby's napkin, the scalpel and forceps of the surgeon, the fisherman's hook; rapidly melting into one another those things which take away from the ancient and painful toil of women, bright-metal taps and screws, electric fittings, radiators, sewing machines, cleaners and wringers, refrigerators; successions of ingenious and intricate machinery and apparatus, knife-edges for balances, delicately adjusted means for measuring and testing; close in my substance as these, great objects of calculated strengths and stresses, steel frames for ships or buildings, engines to take and use the forces of steam and oil and petrol, the heavy wheels of winding and pumping gear, propeller shafts to stand the shock of storms; pulsing through these the hair-springs of watches, finest electrical parts, small objects moving or moved with strictest exactitude. Thus then I knew myself as potentially part of mankind, that extra hand, eye, ear, that ultra-human strength and accuracy which he had made part of his life, of his mastery over and peering into the matter which once mastered him. I knew myself potential giver of the complicated joys and delights which knowledge has given, for all that had been thought into me.

Yet there were other thoughts; there were thoughts of those men who knew that none of this was for them, and my material was heavy with their dumb wonder and resentment, asking a why which I could answer no more than they could. Yet they were trying to answer it, to answer it with hate. Contending thoughts pierced through me, shivering and defacing my images of power. And it began to be plain that none of these potentialities of mine were wholly good; all could be turned into instruments and objects of possession and envy and the power of one sort of man over another. It was borne in upon me that men were forever crossing one another's purposes, so that even the dumb ingots were to them only objects for the working of their malicious and destructive wills. Nor was it known to me in what way I was to be used.

So, after a time of waiting, it came about that my ingots were lifted and piled and taken again to furnaces and forced between rollers, and I knew that at last the wills of men were having effect on me and soon I should get my shape. Then for a time I was a heavy and enormous cylinder, but that was pierced, and spirals were welded into me, and a part of me became careful and intricate machinery and a part of me became supports and great wheels, and all of me shone and glittered with newness and I was a finished thing. During all this process I had become so concerned for my shaping that I was unaware of my purpose, but, as my material essence cooled and slowed and settled, the thoughts of men lighted upon me again. And I became aware that I was a great gun; I became aware that the destructive will had taken me completely; I became aware that my potentials had been taken not for life and delight and use, but only for death. My muzzle pointed inexorably towards death; all parts of me were designed and perfected towards death-giving. And with that, with the heaping of death-thoughts upon me, my awareness began to fade out and grow cold and earth-fixed, metal-fixed, for one purpose only. The shapes of power and ingenuity and beauty and ease-giving had left me now. It was again as though I were the ore deep-hidden and untouched under the earth. Dead and dark.

And out of death and darkness I came to myself slowly in the witch's cave of Soria Moria castle; slowly, slowly my senses un-stiffened, my eyes to sight of the cauldron, my ears to the low crackling of the fire, the low clicking of the knitting needles, my judgement to the knowledge that there was no fourth choice. The witch looked up from her knitting and nodded to me. "You've been a long time," she said. It seemed to me that there was no answer I could give; I only knew that everything should have been different and I knew also that the kind of castle that we build is from its foundations conditioned by the kind of person whom we have allowed ourselves to become. Nor did it seem to me likely that I should ever again bring back reports to that committee upon the nature and substance of any reality.

There was now in that cavernous place an ever more immediate triangle of lines of force, increasingly positive, between myself and the witch and the still dreadfully fuming cauldron. Out against them I set every strength I had of repulsion and courage; yet the basis had been undermined and I was become weak with the despair of the wasted bread and wine and iron. So, step by step, I was drawn nearer to the base of the dreadful triangle, scarcely now against my will but against what I could only know that my will should have been. And the witch took another knife out of her cupboard.

But, as I was almost within reach of her, there came a great noise and a vibration round us, not only in the close air but in the very walls of the castle, and here and there a flake dropt off and fell softly to the floor. And the witch said: "Now, if that isn't provoking! That nasty sea is coming in and we shall have to take to the back-stairs." And with that she opened a peculiar door which had, until then, not been apparent, and, taking her murrey-coloured stockings, which were now of a length beyond any stockings I had seen elsewhere, over the crook of her elbow, she bustled through it, and I, after a moment's hesitation, followed her, for again there had come the shock and the noise of roaring and beating against the castle walls.

Behind the peculiar door was only a great darkness and a stillness beyond any exterior vibration and such that our own footfalls and our own hushed breathing became of an almost unbearable nature, stirring an air that should have been eternally quiescent. Through this, then, we went down and down, and the darkness pressed upon my open eyes and clung round my pushing face and shoulders, and after a time even the shuffling footsteps of the witch were not to be heard, but only my own. It was then that my hands, groping as ever for the wall of the back-staircase, encountered nothing, and it began to come to me, at first slowly and then with an intensely rapid realisation, that this before my eyes, which I had still taken for darkness, was, in its upper part all pierced with stars, which, because of their stillness, I had not been apprehending, and, in its lower part, it was banded with moving and swirling whiteness upon a grey or dark background. And, looking more fully upon this, it became at once apparent that here were the incoming waves.

So, rapidly adjusting myself to these conditions, I perceived that the sea was sufficiently near and was, indeed, about to destroy my carefully made castle. Yet this was of no consequence to me, for to-morrow I should build another and better castle which would in its turn come to destruction and a levelling out of walls below the salt quick water. And in about half an hour, it was high tide.

KATE CRACKERNUTS

LIST OF CHARACTERS
Kate
Ann, *her elder stepsister*
Kate's Mother
The Hen-Wife
Maidens
Sick Prince
Well Prince
Porter
Fairies
A Fairy Baby

ACT I

SCENE I

A corner of a hall in Those Days. Plain walls, a chest or two, a spinning wheel, two stools. On the stools ANN and her younger stepsister KATE, sitting and sewing in bright colours.

Ann:
Stepsister Kate, you sew so fine,
Dear little stitches, all in a line!

Kate:

    I can't sew as somebody can,
    Stepsister Ann, stepsister Ann!

Ann:

    Stepsister Kate, I love you dear,
    All the morning your voice I hear,
    Merry about the household ways,
    Making a pleasure of all the days.

Kate:

    I love you and I love you well,
    This is the prettiest thing to tell:
    Love you more than I'll e'er love man,
    Stepsister Ann, stepsister Ann!

    (They go on sewing. But after a moment Ann sighs
    and passes a hand across her face, letting the sewing lie.)

    What is the thing that clouds your brow?
    Stepsister Ann, what grieves you now?

Ann:

    Oh I am troubled, yes I am troubled,
      Kate, oh Kate, I will tell you how!
    If but your mother were mine own mother,
      I were as happy as bird on bough,
    But oh your mother is my stepmother,
      And there is the trouble that's on me now!

Kate (frowning):

    Well I know that her jealous eye

Watches ever to peep and spy,
Well I know that her jealous heart
Will not give you a daughter's part.
Yet, my Ann, be merry and see
The sunshine dancing—and why not we!

Ann:

Yesternoon when that sun was hot,
I gathered herbs in the garden plot,
By she passed with a baleful look—
Oh I trembled and oh I shook!
Down dropt the basket, down dropt I,
As she looked me full with her glittering eye—
For oh your mother is my stepmother
And there's the reason I pine and sigh!

Kate:

Cheerly Ann! For she will not dare
Hurt or charm you while I am there!
Hush, I hear her foot on the stair!

(*Enter the WICKED STEPMOTHER.*)

Stepmother:

Well, my girls, so your needles run,
Seams all ready by set of sun!
(*To Kate*)
Come, my Kate, I have news for you
Of the finest things to see and to do.
We must give him the best of cheer,
To-morrow the King comes hunting here,

He shall be welcomed with glove and ring
And my daughter Kate shall dance with the King!

Kate:

Oh my mother, here's news that's fine!
Ann, did you hear it, sister mine?
The King is coming to-morrow morn,
The King is coming with hound and horn!
The hounds shall bay and the bells shall ring
And you and I shall dance with the King!

Stepmother (angrily):

What are you saying, Kate, my child!
Your mind's in folly, your words are wild!
You, my daughter, my everything,
Only *you* shall dance with the King!

(Kate jumps up, throwing down her sewing.)

Kate:

Ann, my Ann, is as bonny as I,
Her foot is as light and her head as high,
Her hair as yellow, her eyes as blue
I will not dance unless Ann does too!

Stepmother:

How now, Kate! Shalt do as I say!
I shall order and you obey.
Silence, girl, to my yes or no!

(She turns with a stamp to Ann.)

Ugly Ann, to your chamber go!

Ann (sobbing):
> But oh stepmother, and oh stepmother,
> Why must you speak to hurt me so!
> *(She goes out weeping.)*

Kate (angrily):
> Why must you send my Ann away,
> Why be harsh to her, mother, say?
> For I love my Ann like a true, true sister,
> I love my Ann in work and play!

Stepmother:
> Hush now, Kate, from the closet bring
> Your finest silks to dance with the King,
> Cloth of silver and gold so rare.
> Go, my Kate, I will find you there.

> *(Kate goes out sulkily. The Stepmother speaks with
> great violence and fists clenched.)*

> Ungrateful girls, by your folly led,
> Folly and spite of heart and tongue,
> Ere another day from the earth be fled
> You shall both be sorry for what you have said.
> For the charm will be chanted, the spell be sung,
> And well and truly my plan be sped!
> Hen-wife! . . .

> *(She walks up and down the room muttering to herself.)*

> Hen-wife's magic, help me now,
> Evil magic on field and plough,

Evil magic on hearth and fire,
Evil magic on beast and byre,
Evil magic on woman or man,
And evil's worst on my stepchild Ann!

> (Enter the HEN-WIFE, an old bundle of rags,
> speaking fast.)

Hen-Wife:
Mistress, I'm coming,
Mistress, I'm here,
Past bolt and lock,
I left the drumming
Of my turkey cock,
My ducks so dear,
My geese a gobbling,
My cocks and hens,
My little chickens,
My old dog hobbling,
My coops and pens—

Stepmother (interrupting):
Silence woman, and hearken well,
This is the thing I have to tell:
Do me a magic, lay me a spell,
Make and put, as a Hen-wife can,
An evil charm on my stepchild Ann!

Hen-Wife:
How shall I lay it,
Mistress mine,

What of evil
My spells entwine?
You've but to say it!

Stepmother:
Something ugly upon her lay,
That shall make good people turn away,
Turn and mutter or turn and mock,
And drive out Ann for a laughing stock!

Hen-Wife:
Ann must come knocking
On the Hen-wife's gate,
The clock tick-tocking
At half-past eight
Of a morn of sorrow,
Of a Friday morning
—And that's to-morrow—
The spell will be laid,
Bitter and lasting
In sun or shade,
But I give you warning
To send her fasting!

Stepmother:
On Friday morning at half-past eight
Ann shall come knocking at the Hen-wife's
    gate,
And that's to-morrow!
She shall come fasting, no stop nor stay;

An evil lasting upon her lay
Beyond to-morrow!

Hen-Wife (chuckling):
She shall lift the lid
Of the Hen-wife's pot,
A thing shall be hid
In my stew so hot,
In my stew so deep,
Out it shall leap
And long may she rue it!
I will not stay me
But up and do it,
My spell threads twine.

   (whining)

Mistress of mine,
How will you pay me?

Stepmother:
In yonder chest is a purse of gold,
That shall be yours when the tale is told.

Hen-Wife:
I will be going,
I will away,
Past door and lock,
Back to the crowing
Of my crested cock,
My ducks a-dabbling,
My hens a-laying,

My geese a-gabbling,
My chicks a-playing,
My turkeys too,
Back to my cottage
And the Hen-wife's brew!

(*She goes out.*)

Stepmother:
So to-morrow morning I shall work my plan
And there'll be an end of my stepdaughter Ann!

SCENE II

The same room. The next morning. Ann, Kate and the Stepmother.

Stepmother:
The cooks are busy, the tables gay
For the feast we give for the King to-day,
Candles to burn and herbs to strew.
Stepdaughter Ann, here's work for you:
Take up your cloak and your basket brown,
To the Hen-wife's gate go quickly down,
For my cakes must have—and without delay!—
All the eggs that her hens can lay.

Ann:
Here is my cloak and basket brown;
Fasting I'll go to the Hen-wife down,

And only ask—and be scarce delayed—
A sup of curds from the dairy-maid.

Stepmother (sharply):
    The maid is busy, the dairy locked,
    Go now, Ann, I will not be mocked!
    We will eat and drink, and of cream no lack,
    Cakes and junkets when Ann comes back!

        (She laughs grimly. Ann goes out.)

Kate (sings. Air: "Sing a Song of Sixpence."):
    Roses, roses, we must strew
        Where the King's to come to-day.

        (Enter maids with flowers.)

    You and you and you and you,
        Petals, petals, all the way!

        *(All of them strew flowers about the room, while
        Kate sings. This should be made to last a fairly long
        time.)*

    Here are pinks and here are fine.
        Striped carnations, sweet and hot.
    Make your pansies' faces shine!
        Here is tasselled bergamot.
    Blue of borage, green of box,
        Silver gold of dropping lime,
    Royal purple spikes of stocks,
        Make a carpet, make a rhyme.

Bring me lilies, hot with sun,
  Leaf and star of jasmine bring,
Through the castle leap and run,
  Make a pathway for the King!

  (*They go out, still dancing, leaving Kate and
  Stepmother.*)

Stepmother (*to herself*):
  Now the clock's at half-past eight,
  Ann will be knocking at the Hen-wife's gate.
  She will be taken in the Hen-wife's plot,
  She will lift the lid of the Hen-wife's pot!
  The smoke will stink and the stew will reek,
  Ann will find something she did not seek!
    (*She laughs.*)

Kate:
  Why are you laughing, mother, mother,
  With a grim, grim look in your eyes coming after? You
    look so strange to me, mother, mother,
  I am afraid when I hear your laughter!

  (*Re-enter Ann, with a sheep's-head in place of her
  own head. She stumbles and holds out her hands and
  bleats. Kate does not for a moment recognize her.*)

Stepmother:
  Here comes the working of the Hen-wife's plan!

Kate:
  What are you? Why are you? Who are you? Ann!
  (*She runs to her. Ann bleats again.*)

What has come to you, dear, my dear?
What the charm, with your Kate not near?
Ann that I love like my true, true sister,
Do not tremble and do not fear!

Stepmother:
Sheep's-head Ann, in the time that's past,
We see in her own true shape at last!
Come away Kate, there's naught to miss,
You shall have better friends than this!
   (She claps her hands and shoos Ann away.)
Bleat at me, sheep-nose, all you can,
Off to the byres with sheep's-head Ann!

Kate (taking Ann's hand in hers and holding it tight):
Ann, I know you, I love you still,
I shall help you with heart and will!
I shall go with you, never fear,
I'll be your sister, Ann, my dear!

Stepmother (sharply):
Kate, from the sheep's-head take your hand!
Off, away from the sheep's-head stand!
Leave her, go from her, off to the wall,
Or the sheep's-head curse on you shall fall!

   (Ann bleats.)

Kate:
Now I know why you laughed so queerly,
Now I know why you looked so grim,

Mother that once I loved so dearly,
Mother I hate now, nearly, nearly—
   Ah, how the light goes dim, goes dim!
Mother, I see the dark immerse you,
   Go your ways from it if you can,
Ere a coffin of evil hearse you—
Mother, I go before I curse you,
   Mother, I go with my sister Ann!

   *(She takes a veil from the chest and wraps it round
Ann's head, while her mother stands trembling. Then
she and Ann go out together.)*

Stepmother:
   Oh she is gone, my Kate, my Kate,
   Gone with curses and gone with hate,
      Gone on the storm like a rose in bloom,
   She would not stay, and she would not wait,
      I see my deed and I see my doom
   And I see myself too late, too late!

   (As she stands there, the Hen-wife comes in again.)

Hen-Wife:
   The purse of gold,
   The purse of gold,
      For me to gloat on,
   To have and hold,
      For me to dote on!
   The tale's well told

Of the Hen-wife's magic,
The Hen-wife's curse.
Mistress, the purse!
Mistress, the gold!

    (The Stepmother goes to the chest and takes out a purse of gold.)

Stepmother:

I swore to pay you and pay I will.

    (She flings the purse in her face. The coins scatter.)

Go in evil and go in ill!
Go in storm, in sleet and in rain,
So I never look on your face again!

ACT II

SCENE I

    The gate of a castle. Either the whole gate, or a wicket in it, should be made to open. There is a small window at the side which should open too. Kate and Ann come in, both wearing cloaks. Ann still has the linen web wrapped round her head.

    Kate: Here's a castle, dearest. We shall get food and lodging for to-night, and to-morrow will come when it must. Are you tired, Ann?

    (Ann bleats.)

A little tired? Well, so am I.

(She knocks on the door.)

No answer, no answer to poor folk like Kate and Ann!
Well, I must needs sing for our supper.

(She sings: Air: "Lavender's Blue.")

Roses are red, dilly, dilly, lavender's blue,
Where I can go, dilly, dilly, Ann shall come too.
If in the hall, dilly, dilly, if on the stair,
If at the feast, dilly, dilly, Ann shall be there!
If I have bread, dilly, dilly, if I have wine,
If I have meat, dilly, dilly, Ann shall have mine!

*(The small window opens and the WELL PRINCE
looks out of it: feathered cap and tunic, etc. Kate looks up;
Ann buries her veiled head in her arms.)*

Well Prince:
    Who are you, beggar girls, standing there?
      You with the cloak and the bold brown eyes,
    You with the veil over face and hair
      And the trembling look of a bird that flies,
    A bird afraid that has seen the snare!

Kate: Why, we are beggar girls, as you say. We want
food and a night's lodging. Are you a Prince?

Well Prince:
    I am a Prince, bold beggar maid,
    But a sorry prince, and a prince betrayed,

A prince betrayed by a spite of fate
And a sore, sore trouble upon me laid.

Kate: Why, we have had troubles, too, I and my sister.
I know about troubles. What is yours?

Well Prince:

I had a brother, who once was gay,
Merry and brave as a colt in May,
But once he was caught by the Green Hill people
Who turned him dour and fierce and fey.
His touch is fever, his looks are grim
His feet are heavy, his eyes are dim,
And all because of the Green Hill people
Who cast their luring, their spell on him!
By day he hides from the light of the sun,
He eats but little, he speaks to none,
But at night he goes to the Green Hill people
To dance in the hill till the dark is done.

Kate: You should have a watcher with him at night, a
strong and careful watcher who is not afraid of the Green
Hill people nor of any magic.

Well Prince:

Many a one has stayed at night
To watch by his bed till the morning light,
But every watcher has vanished, vanished,
Magicked away from human sight!
Magicked away by the Green Hill people

Who laugh at loving or faith or right!
And my brother laughs, he laughs in the morning,
With eyes all shadowed and cheeks all white.

Kate: It is a sad thing to hear that kind of laughter. I
have heard laughter that bit at my heart. Well then, prince,
are we to have shelter in your castle? Must I sing again?

Well Prince:
Sing, bold maiden, and cheer my heart!
    (to Ann)
And you with the hands that flutter and start,
Will you lift the veil and show your beauty,
Your eyes that kindle and looks that dart?

(Ann shrinks and turns away.)

Kate (sings. Air: *"Over the Water to Charlie"):*
My sister Ann was good as gold,
    My sister Ann was bonny,
Dear to kiss and fine to hold,
    As sweet as bread and honey.
A cruel spell on her was laid
    Upon her face so bonny,
Although she was a gentle maid
    And sweet as bread and honey.
So no man now her face may see,
    Nor kiss her lips so bonny,
Though he were a King of Araby,
    Or good as bread and honey!

Well Prince:
> You shall sing again, for I must know more.
> For your sister's sake my heart is sore,
> I will away and bid the porter,
> Slip back the bolts of my castle door!

> *(He goes from the window.)*

Kate: Well, dearest, there's a sad prince!

> *(Ann bleats.)*

A sad prince, but a handsome one, you say? Well, maybe. But at least he is giving us shelter at the end of a long day. If only we could stay here and not wear out those pretty feet of yours on the hard roads!

> *(Ann bleats.)*

Not worn out? No, but they will be. And so will mine ! Now tell me, Ann, what do you say to this: that I go watch this sick prince at nights and get good pay for it?

> *(Ann bleats and catches at Kate's hands.)*

Silly Ann, there's nothing to fear. 'Tis not your sister Kate will vanish away in smoke for a little watching! It will take more than a spell from any Green Hill people to magic your Kate away!

> *(Ann bleats.)*

Hush, here's the porter, we'll see what he says to it.

(The gate opens and the PORTER looks out; he is an important little man in red.)

Porter:
> I am Peter Porter,
> The castle Porter,
> I open the door in
> The stones and mortar,
> Let three or four in,
> Ladies a-riding
> Or knights in armour,
> A lovely charmer,
> Or a captain striding.
> I'm Peter Porter!
> I let them all in,
> Taller or shorter,
> Beggar or gypsy,
> I bid them crawl in,
> Sober or tipsy!
> I'm Peter Porter,
> And a curtsy, please—
> The Prince has the castle,
> But I have the keys!

Kate: Mr. Peter Porter, your servants!

(She and Ann curtsy.)

Porter: The Prince bade me let you in, but 'tis I have the passing of you. What work will you do, beggar maids?

Kate: I can do most things about a house, and what I've not done yet I can try my hand at.

Porter: There's but one piece of work needs doing in this castle, and that needs a stouter heart than any beggar maid can put to it.

Kate: Maybe I can guess the work you mean. I could be a sick-bed watcher, Mr. Peter Porter. *(Ann tugs at her hand.)* No, Ann, I must ask! Tell me, Mr. Peter Porter, what reward would a girl get who watched all night with your sick prince?

(As she says this the SICK PRINCE comes to the window and looks down, watching them, dark and smiling, bareheaded with a wild lock coming down over the forehead.)

Porter: Mistress beggar maid, the pay that is offered to man or woman who watches a night with the sick prince is a whole peck of silver.

Kate: Why, I could spend that with a light heart! I need new shoe-laces! Mr. Peter Porter, what kind of a prince is this sick prince of yours?

Porter (with a sideways glance): You've but to look at the window, mistress beggar maid, and you'll see.

(Kate looks up. The Sick Prince laughs.)

Ah, he knows you'll go the same way the others went.

Kate: But all the same, I'll do it.

(Ann bleats.)

Porter (startled): What was that?

Kate: Nothing at all. I will watch your sick prince for you.

(At this the Sick Prince goes from the window.)

Bring us in, Mr. Peter Porter. When I have my peck of silver, you shall have something out of it.

Porter: Come then, beggar maids.

(He goes in, followed by Ann. Kate still stands for a moment, staring at the window.)

Kate:
This is the thing I have waited for,
This is the thing I left my home for,
All I have loved and hated for,
All that I ever thought to roam for!
Oh prince, sick prince, I will be your healer,
I will be bold as I am bonny,
I will go to the fairy hill,
I will be listener, I will be stealer,
I will dare go down through the black, black mould,
Under the turf of the fairy hill.
If I am bonny, I will be bold,
I will follow my prince to the fairy hill.
I will set my will to the will of the fairies,
A mortal will to the fairy will,

I will follow my prince and keep and hold,
And bring him back from the fairy hill!

(*She turns and goes into the castle, after the Porter
and sister Ann.*)

SCENE II

(*The Sick Prince's room in the castle. A chest, a stool by
the fire, a low bed spread with a green silken cover. The
Sick Prince stands at the window, holding back the curtain
and looking out.*)

Sick Prince:
Sleep . . . I will sleep now . . . I will sleep and sleep.
Soon I must rise and ride. The sky is steep,
I must tread down the stars. Oh set of sun,
In the Green Hill the dancing has begun!
They wait for me. At midnight I will go.

(*He turns from the window.*)

All day the hours drag, the clocks are slow;
My brother and the rest would have me gay,
They'd have me laughing all the hateful day!
They talk; they give me food I cannot eat,
They slink about my ways, they lie, they cheat,
I hate their spying looks, their service bought!
And I am hindered, hindered from the thought
Of fairy gladness, fairy wine and bread,

That lovely light about the Green Hill shed,
The thick, close sweetness of the fairy hill!
Oh how I hate these mortals that must still
Press all about me, touch me, drag me back
To the hot slavering of the human pack,
Hold me, possess me, catch me, make me well,
A well, glad devil in the human hell!
They say another's come to watch to-night,
I hate the thought of her, the touch, the sight.
Ah fairies, catch her, hold her in the hill,
Set your fine wills against her mortal will,
This gold-bought human in your green hill keep!
Sleep . . . I will sleep now . . . I will sleep and sleep.

*(He lies down on the green bed and goes to sleep.
Music. After a little time the Porter comes in, on
tiptoe.)*

Porter *(speaking over his shoulder)*:
Yes, yes, come in!

*(Kate and Ann come in, looking from him to the
sleeping prince.)*

He is like this always in the evening. Dead asleep. It is
only later that he wakes. As the clock strikes midnight.

Kate (bending over him): Poor lad, poor lad. He is
dreaming of the fairies. Well, if there is nothing left of me
to-morrow morning, you shall give the peck of silver to my
sister Ann!

(*Ann bleats*)

Porter: What was that?

Kate: Nothing at all. Give me the stool, Mr. Peter Porter. I will sit there and sing myself awake all night.

(*The Porter draws the stool forward. Enter the Well Prince.*)

Well Prince:
So you have come, brave beggar maid,
Knowing the peril, but not afraid!
Welcome to you and your bonny sister
With the grey veil still o'er her bright eyes laid!

Kate: It is I, not she, who will do the watching. Goodnight, Ann, good-night, my dear. (*They kiss*) Wish me well and have good dreams. Now go, my Ann.

(*Exeunt Ann and the Porter.*)

Well Prince (looking after Ann):
There she goes with her step so fine,
But I wish I could see her blue eyes shine,
And I wish your sister were my own sister
And I wish her good-night kiss were mine!

Kate: I would sooner see her go to you than to any other man. If she could. If the spell were off her. Prince, if I am magicked away to-night, will you care for my sick sister Ann?

Well Prince:
> If your sick sister were left alone,
> I would not leave her to sigh or moan,
> But I would care for your sad sick sister
> As though your sister had been mine own.

Kate: I will have that in mind through my watching. And now, Prince, you should go. Only wish me luck after midnight in the fairy time.

Well Prince:
> Oh I wish you luck and I wish you well,
> May all good counsel be with you still,
> Oh I wish you well in the Fairy Hill
> And a fine, fine tale at dawn to tell!

> *(He goes out.)*

Kate: Well now, here's time before midnight and a good fire to spend it by. *(She goes over to the Sick Prince.)* He's sleeping sound enough now. I'll sing and keep me awake. *(She sits on the stool and sings. Air: "Lilliburlero.")*

There was a maid that loved a lad
  (The broom is bonny on bank and brae)
A silver penny was all she had
  (And I'll go up to the broom to-day).

The lad was noble, the lad was proud
  (The broom is bonny on bank and brae)
He scorned the maid in a voice so loud
  (And I'll go up to the broom to-day).

He went a-walking to take the air,
    (The broom is bonny on bank and brae)
He went a-walking by the mill dam fair.
    (And I'll go up to the broom to-day).

He went a-walking, as I am told,
    (The broom is bonny on bank and brae)
When by there came a robber bold.
    (And I'll go up to the broom to-day).

That robber took his gold so bright,
    (The broom is bonny on bank and brae)
And bound his hands behind him tight.
    (And I'll go up to the broom to-day).

Proud youth, said he, I'll have your life,
    (The broom is bonny on bank and brae)
I'll slay you with my little pen-knife.
    (And I'll go up to the broom to-day).

But by there came that silly maid,
    (The broom is bonny on bank and brae)
She heard all the bold robber said.
    (And I'll go up to the broom to-day).

She tripped up like any lamb
    (The broom is bonny on bank and brae)
She pushed the robber into the mill dam.
    (And I'll go up to the broom to-day).

That proud lad's hands she straight unbound,
    (The broom is bonny on bank and brae)

And woke him out of his sore swound.
    (And I'll go up to the broom to-day).

He kissed her lips that were so red:
    (The broom is bonny on bank and brae)
"But for you I had been dead"
    (And I'll go up to the broom to-day).

"But for you I had lost my life"
    (The broom is bonny on bank and brae)
"Now you shall be my dear wife."
    (And I'll go up to the broom to-day).

    (She stops singing and speaks.)

There's a silly song! My nurse was used to sing it. And
in the last verse of all they are wedded and live happy ever
after. Well, I'll not sing that. *(She goes over to the Sick
Prince.)* He's asleep still. *(She goes back to the stool.)* Nothing to do but sing again.

    (She sings. Air: "Jacket and Petticoat.")

As I went by with my sister Ann,
I saw a middling fine young man,
Middling fine, middling fine,
I saw a middling fine young man!

As I looked up and as I walked in
Then he looked down and gave me a grin,
Gave me a grin, gave me a grin,
Oh he looked down and gave me a grin!

As I sat there on my little chair,
That fine young man . . .

*(She breaks off as the clock strikes twelve. On the twelfth
stroke the Sick Prince sits up on his bed.)*

Sick Prince:
Yes, I am coming! Yes, the dance is set.
In the Green Hill the company is met . . .
Oh I can hear the thin long notes that come
Across the muffled beating of the drum,
The heavy drum, the fairy drum, the luring
Drum that has set a dance time there's no curing,
A dance time in my head and in my heart.
Now down! To horse, to horse! The pipers start,
In the Green Hill where such fine folks are met.
Yes, I am coming, yes, the dance is set!

(He gets up and goes out. Kate follows him silently.)

SCENE III

*Inside the Green Hill. Green light, green curtains, pulled
back to make a cavern. The Fairies are dancing under the
slope of the hill: green and brown, or green and silver dresses,
pointed caps, slanted eyes. On one side stand two Fairies who
play the dance tune, one with a recorder or some wood wind
instrument, the other with a small drum. On the other side
stands a Fairy who sings. Either the singing is continuous
throughout the dancing or else there is first a verse sung dur-*

ing the dance and then the dance goes on while the tune is played through once more, rather louder, by the recorder and drum. Then the singing and dancing together, then the dancing alone. The tune is "Linten Lowring," with the four lines of the chorus played rather rapidly. During the slow first half of the air, the Fairies dance weavingly, lifting their arms slowly and high, with dragging steps, but during the quick second half they run in and out in a rapid chain, or under arches of joined hands.

Fairy (singing. Air: "Linten Lowring."):
>   For miles and miles the nut groves lie,
>   From bush to bush the robins flit,
>   The Fairy Hill is in the midst
>   With green grass growing over it.
>   Up and under, in and under,
>   Down and under, well or ill,
>   You'll go the way you shouldna' go
>   And find yourself in the Fairy Hill!
>   And who would know or who would guess
>   What plays are played, what songs are sung
>   Behind the lovely hazel groves
>   Where all the Spring the catkins swung?
>   Up and under, in and under,
>   Down and under, well or ill,
>   You'll go the way you shouldna' go
>   And find yourself in the Fairy Hill!

(Enter the Sick Prince, quickly, through the swinging green of the curtains. Behind him Kate follows quietly; she has her

apron full of nuts, caught up in one hand. The tune goes on, encircling and drawing away the Prince, who takes hands with the Fairies and follows them into the dance. Kate stands, upright, pressed back against the green wall, staring and watching as they dance.)

Fairy (singing):
> And he who once has seen the dance
> Will surely come, will come again,
> And she who seeks to hinder him
> She toils in vain, she toils in vain.
> Up and under, in and under,
> Down and under, well or ill,
> He's gone the way he shouldna' go
> And found himself in the Fairy Hill!

(They dance with him for another round of the tune, then the music stops, with the Fairies grouped round the Prince, all looking sidelong at Kate.)

Fairy (speaks):
> What's to do and where to go,
> Shall we take her, shall we keep her?
> In the harvest of the foe
> Shall we bind her, shall we reap her?
> In the Green Hill deeper
> Shall we stack her, hold her, keep her?

Sick Prince (with hate):
> Take her, take her,
> Bind her, blind her!

In the dancing lose her, make her
Give up striving, give up hoping!
Leave her groping
Full of pain,
Fairy pains that rack and shake her,
Out and up and all in vain!

Kate:

Oh my Prince, who is bound, so bound,
Whose heart must hate and whose look would kill,
I will bring you living and whole and sound,
Oh kinder-eyed on to mortal ground,
And back with me from the Fairy Hill!

*(The dance tune begins again. Some of the Fairies dance
away and out of sight with the Sick Prince, while others
come nearer and nearer to Kate, holding out their arms to
her.)*

Fairies (singing):

Did you but know what joys were here,
For Kate, for Kate, our dearest Kate,
You needs must love the Fairy Hill,
You would not hate, you could not hate!
Up and under, in and under,
Down and under, well or ill,
You've gone the way you shouldna' go
And found yourself in the Fairy Hill!

*(Kate takes a step forward in spite of herself, as she does
so dropping and scattering the nuts from her apron. The*

Fairies take her hands and pull her into the middle of their circle but there she snatches herself away from them and crouches, her hands over her ears, while they dance round her.)

Fairies (singing):
    Would you but join the fairy dance,
    Oh sweetest sweet—your Prince's hate
    Would turn to love, would turn to love
    For Kate, his Kate, for fairy Kate!
    Up and under, in and under,
    Down and under, well or ill,
    You've gone the way you shouldna' go
    And found yourself in the Fairy Hill!

(Kate jumps to her feet in the midst of the circle, crying out against the Fairy tune.)

Kate:
    Stop your dancing and hush your song,
    It has rung in my ears too long, too long!
    Sweet is dancing and sweet is love,
    But I must remember the world above!
    It went to my heart so deep, so deep,
    But a fairy promise is ill to keep,
    And I'll not harvest with Green Hill people
    And I'll not stack where the fairies reap!

(The Fairies gather at one side, laughing spitefully and pointing their fingers at her.)

Fairies (laughing):
  Foolish mortal, foolish human,
  Where's the profit for a woman
  But in dancing, but in singing,
  Clasping fingers, fondly swinging,
  Flinging, ringing,
  In our dancing,
  Once you pass the Green Hill's portal,
  Foolish woman, foolish mortal!

  (They go out, still laughing, to another round of the dance tune. The Fairy singers and players follow them out and, while Kate is alone, the tune is heard faintly and fitfully from behind the scene.)

  Kate *(with a deep sigh)*: So! And I might have gone with them . . . and danced . . . and never seen my Ann again. They'll let me be now. Oh that tune. It's in my head for ever.

  (She sings to the second half of the tune faintly sounding from beyond.)

  Up and under, in and under,
  Down and under, well or ill.
  We went the way we shouldna' go,
  And found ourselves in the Fairy Hill.
  He'll be dancing with them now . . . dancing till dawn. And what's poor Kate to do? Well, well, poor Kate can pick up her nuts and crack them.

(She begins to pick up the scattered nuts. Every now and then she cracks one between her teeth and eats it.)

Good mortal food—no fairy stuff, but squirrels' nuts from the hazel bushes. I've robbed you, squirrels! Kate has robbed you . . . Kate Crackernuts. There's a sweet one. Yes, it was a long ride for Kate, a long ride through the hazel woods on the crupper of his horse, and he in a dream, not noticing. Oh that tune . . . how I could have danced with him! Next time—if there is a next time—I shall hide when I follow him in. I'll not have them luring me again. I might have danced . . . oh, I might have danced!

(Again the dance tune sounds from behind. Perhaps the lights should be lowered here to show the passing of the time towards the dawn. Kate cracks her nuts, humming the tune to herself. But suddenly the tune goes louder again, and the Fairies and the Sick Prince come dancing in. Kate presses back into the folds of the green curtains.)

Fairies (singing):
    The dawn is on the hazel groves,
    Where long the dewy shadows lie.
    Until the midnight chimes again
    Our Prince, good-bye—our Prince, good-bye.
    Up and under, in and under,
    Down and under, well or ill,
    You'll go the way you shouldna' go
    And find yourself in the Fairy Hill!

*(As the song ceases they drop away from him sleepily,
some kneeling upright still, but others sinking and curling
to the ground all round him and pillowing their faces in
their hands.)*

Fairy (speaks):
Oh foolish morning,
Oh red-faced sun,
Spoiling our dancing,
Staring and scorning,
Striding and prancing,
As though you'd never
Be ended and done,
You hindering, blundering, mortal sun!

*(The Fairy yawns and stretches and sinks down into
sleep among the others, at the Prince's feet. He stands
among them and speaks.)*

Sick Prince:
Dawn . . . and the weary ride, the long ride back
Among the hazels, down the winding track.
How fleet I rode at midnight when the stars
Peered blinkingly between the branches' bars,
Watched me beneath low hazel arches flitting
—And her, the woman on my crupper sitting!—
I would not shake her off, I did not care.
What's it to me—these mortals—though they dare
Follow and spy, creeping beneath the moon?
The fairies' vengeance will be on her soon!

Oh nothing matters, nothing but the singing,
The night-long dances through the green hill swinging,
The tingling link of hands, the faery light
That glows beneath the turf all night, all night.
My pulse beats to the dance tune, quick or slow,
Oh cruel dawn, to check the ebb and flow!
Dawn . . . I must say the words that bid me go.

*(He takes a step clear of the Fairies, lifts his hands towards
the green wall and speaks commandingly.)*

Open, open, Green Hill, and let the Prince go through!

*(He takes a step through the curtains and out. Kate
steps quickly from her hiding place and follows him.)*

Kate:
And his lady him behind!

*(She too goes out from the Hill, leaving the Fairies
asleep.)*

ACT III

SCENE I

*A room in the castle. Ann sitting on a stool, still with
the veil over her sheep's-head, peeling carrots into a crockery bowl. The Porter comes in and wags a finger over her.*

Porter:
> Your sister has vanished,
> I told you she would!

> *(Ann bleats and drops her carrots.)*

> Now, none of that squealing,
> It does you no good!
> Get on with those carrots
> You ought to be peeling!
> Your sister has vanished,
> I told you she would.
> Your duties to-day are,
> (No squeaking I pray!) are:
> First finish those carrots,
> And then feed the pike,
> And then feed the rabbits,
> And then feed the parrots
> Whose curious habits
> I know you will like.
> You must brush every feather,
> Each red and green feather,
> And pray do it neatly!
> Your sister has vanished,
> Has vanished completely,
> And nothing whatever
> Will do the least good.
> Your sister has vanished,
> I told you she would!

(*Ann drops her head in her hands and bleats despairingly. The Porter continues.*)

I flatter myself I can put beggar maids in their places! I have the manner. She will now attend to the Call of Duty.

(*As he pats himself assertively on the chest, the Well Prince comes in and over to Ann.*)

Well Prince:
In my brother's room the light is dim,
Silence stays in it deep and grim.
He has gone again to the Green Hill people
And your sister Kate has gone with him.
On my poor brother the spell lies true,
Nothing's to help and naught to do;
But Ann, poor Ann, you have lost your sister
Who was more than all of the world to you!

(*Ann gets to her feet, wringing her hands and bleating piteously.*)

Yet you must hope for another day,
Yet you must listen to what I say:
Ann, you must speak to your Prince who loves you,
Ann, you must take your veil away!

(*He lays his hand on the veil to tear it away from Ann's face; she bleats wildly, catching at his wrists to stop him.*)

Porter (*with satisfaction*): Ah, that's the way to treat these beggar girls!

(As they are struggling Kate comes in behind them.)

Kate: What, Prince! Here's no way to make a poor girl fond of you!

(He lets go of Ann, who sobs in Kate's arms.)

There, my Ann, I'm back safe and sound. It takes more than a fairy to steal your sister! Or a fairy tune . . . My Prince is sound asleep on his bed, a long sleep after his long ride. Yes, it was a night's work, watching him! I shall sleep all day. Will you give Ann the peck of silver?

Porter: Here it is, mistress beggar maid!

(He fetches it.)

Kate: Spread your apron, Ann!

(Ann spreads her apron and the Porter pours in the peck of silver.)

I got nothing but nuts out of the woods in my apron. I am Kate Crackernuts, and now you are Ann Rainsilver!

Well Prince:
Kate, oh Kate, who has watched aright,
Whose eye is proud as her step is light,
Will you fetch him back from the Green Hill people,
Will you watch my brother another night?

Kate: Yes, I will watch, but not for the same price. This time, Prince, I must have a peck of gold.

Porter (scandalized): There's a greedy beggar girl!

Well Prince:
>She shall have that and welcome too,
>For what is gold when the heart must rue?
>And what is gold to my own, own brother,
>Now I have found a watcher true!

>*(The Prince and the Porter go out. Kate holds Ann in her arms and speaks over her bowed head.)*

Kate:
>Ann shall have silver and Ann shall have gold,
>Dresses and jewels to fondle and hold,
>Gold and silver and her heart's desire,
>Ann shall sit at her own hearth fire.
>Hen-wife's magic shall not endure
>When Ann's own sister shall seek a cure.
>The sheep's-head curse shall tumble away,
>Sister Kate will not let it stay!
>For sister Kate as a sister can
>Shall be a good sister to sister Ann.

SCENE II

The Fairy Hill. The Fairies are dancing as before, to the same tune, but there should be some variation in the dance itself.

Fairies (singing):
> Below the hot, the steady blue
> The thick-leaved woods lay calm all day,
> But now the hooves tread down the grass,
> The hazel boughs divide and sway.
> Up and under, in and under,
> Down and under, well or ill,
> He'll go the way he shouldna' go
> And find himself in the Fairy Hill!
> Oh gladdening strong his mortal limbs
> And steely sweet his mortal glance,
> Who comes to find below the hill
> His fairy partners in the dance.
> Up and under, in and under,
> Down and under, well or ill,
> He'll go the way he shouldna' go
> And find himself in the Fairy Hill!

(Enter the Sick Prince and Kate immediately behind him. But Kate hides so quickly between the folds of the green curtain that the Fairies do not see her.)

Fairy (speaks):
> Did she come, did she follow,
> The mortal maiden,
> By hill and hollow
> Of the nut groves fair?
> Or did you ride on

A horse unladen
Through the midnight air?

Sick Prince (strangely):
I do not know,
Fairies.
She is kind and gentle,
With silence shod.
I can hardly hate her.
She is cool as snow,
Strong and supple as hazel,
As a tall hazel rod.
There is no art, no magic,
Her kindness to enhance.
I cannot tell if she came with me, fairies!
Come, let us dance.

Fairy (rapidly):
Forget, forget her,
She is kind with a purpose,
A mortal purpose,
Do not let, do not let her
Break the spell,
Break the tune!
All's well
Under stars and moon,
Hear and tell,
Come soon!
Now the dance, the dance, the dance and the dance
tune!

(*The Fairies begin to dance again, sweeping the Prince in with them.*)

Fairies (singing):
  Asleep the birds, the foxes sleep,
  In hazel coverts sleeps the fawn,
  Forget, forget the mortal world
  Until the breaking of the dawn.
  Up and under, in and under,
  Down and under, well or ill,
  He's come the way he shouldna' come
  And found himself in the Fairy Hill!

(*The Fairies dance out and away with the Prince. The dance tune sounds faintly. Kate comes out from behind the curtain. She holds up with one hand her apron full of nuts.*)

Kate: He said I was kind . . . that's sweet, sweet hearing. I would be kind to him for always . . . kinder than all the fairies under the world. Kinder and merrier. And maybe his brother would be as kind to my Ann . . . If I could but find a cure for her . . . What's here?

(*She hides again quickly. Two FAIRY WOMEN come in, one carrying a FAIRY BABY. She puts him down on the floor.*)

Fairy Woman: Star-cap, Star-cap, where's thy ball? I plucked him as fine a puff ball as ever lifted its head, grown between sweet dusk and dawn of midsummer night. But babes are ever the best losers, under turf or under roof!

Other Fairy: Give him the wand, Gossip. Star-cap, Star-cap, here's a pretty toy for thee!

(She picks up a bright silver and gold wand, pointed with a crescent moon, and gives it to the baby.)

Fairy Woman: Dost know the power of the wand thou hast given my Star-cap?

Other Fairy: Tell me, Gossip.

Fairy Woman: One stroke of that wand, Gossip, would make Kate Crackernuts' sick sister Ann as hale and bonny as ever she was!

Other Fairy: Then it's well Kate Crackernuts is not here in the Hill, or our wand would be stolen away!

(They go out, leaving the baby playing on the floor with the wand. Kate steps cautiously out from between the folds of the curtain, glances about her, and kneels down on the floor beside the Fairy baby.)

Kate: Can I see thy toy, Star-cap? Show it me then, show it to Kate. Oh, the pretty wand!

(She tries to take it, but the baby will not let it go.)

Look, then, Star-cap—see what Kate has for thee!

(She takes nuts out of her apron and begins to roll them about the floor. The Fairy baby is interested.)

Nuts. Hazel nuts from up above the Hill in the blue
air. Nuts that Kate Crackernuts plucked down for thee
from the brushing branches.

*(The baby begins to play with the nuts, dropping the
wand and leaving it.)*

Shall Kate have thy pretty toy, then? And thou have the
nuts, Star-cap? Look, shalt have them every one.

*(The baby picks up most of the nuts and trots out with
them, leaving Kate with the wand. Kate stands up, holding
it in both hands, triumphantly.)*

I have it, I have it, I have stolen the wand!
 I have set my will to the fairies' and my will has won.
I will get my sister Ann free of her sore, sore bond,
 Out of the cruel web that the Hen-wife's magic
  spun.
Oh bonny the hazel groves and the good pastures
 beyond,
 I will be out and away at the rising of the sun!

*(She hides the wand in the breast of her dress and lis-
tens. Perhaps the lights should go down again now to indi-
cate the passing of time and a few notes of the fairy tune
heard. She speaks, slowly.)*

The Fairy tune again . . . but I am steel against it.
There's no power left in it. I would not dance if I could.
Oh Ann, Ann, Ann, if you but knew how soon you would
be your own bonny self again!

(She darts behind the curtain as the dancers come in again, the Sick Prince in their midst.)

Fairies (singing):

Our dancing feet at dusk leapt up
And oh, we would be dancing more,
But sleep at dawn like mist is laid
All white about the dancing floor.
Up and under, in and under,
Down and under, well or ill,
You'll go the way you shouldna' go
And find yourself in the Fairy Hill!

(The Fairies settle to sleep all about the Prince, one only remaining half upright at his side.)

Fairy (sleepily):

Dawn again the dance has found,
You must leave the fairy ground
And the dancers dreaming
Of a dancing, streaming,
Ribbon of dancing all unbound.

(Then she, too, sinks to the ground in sleep. The Sick Prince looks down at them gently.)

Sick Prince:

Fairies, sleep well, sleep well, my partners dear
In your green cave below the changing year.
The hazels drop their leaves, thin falls the snow:

But winter's nothing to you here below.
Bare twigs and catkins next; and in July
The thick green leaves that prop the thick blue sky.
And now the nuts are ripe, the autumn dew
Drenches the moss-bright turf. But over you
The sweet year passes as an eagle passes,
One high, faint fleck above the moorland grasses.
Sleep well, dear partners, in a gentle flow
Of easy dreaming dancing to and fro.
Dawn . . . I must speak the words that bid me go.

(He steps clear of the Fairies and lifts his hand commandingly towards the green wall.)

Open, open, Green Hill, and let the Prince go through!

(He steps through the curtains and out. Kate follows quickly from her hiding place.)

Kate: And his lady him behind!

(She follows him out of the Hill, leaving the fairies asleep.

SCENE III

A room in the castle, empty. Kate comes in, excited, her hands clasped over the breast of her dress, and the wand.

Kate: Ann? *(She looks all round.)* Ann! Oh, Ann! She doesn't know yet. But I know.

(Ann runs in and up to her, bleating.)

Ann, my sweet, I'm back again. They couldn't stop me, they couldn't stop Kate Crackernuts. And see what I have here, Ann, see what I have here! *(She pulls out wand.)* This tiny, shiny, fairy thing. Ann, let me unwind the veil from your head.

(Ann shakes her head in refusal, bleating.)

No, but let me, Ann! Your Prince shall not see you with the sheep's-head. It is only your sister Kate.

(She unwinds the veil from the sheep's-head and looks at it.)

Now, ugly thing, that has sat thyself on my Ann's bonny shoulders, I'll deal with thee! *(She strikes at it with her wand.)* Off! Off! *(It does not budge.)* What, what, have the fairies cheated me? No, I'll not have it!

(She catches the sheep's-head by the ears and pulls. It comes off and there is Ann herself under it.)

Oh, Ann, is that you again, is that you . . . !

Ann: Oh, Kate . . .

(She gives a little, quick sob, feeling about with her hands. Kate throws the sheep's-head down on to the ground.)

Kate:
>   I went to the Fairy Hill
>   To heal and steal and be wise.

I looked in the fairy eyes
And I set my human will
Not to dance, not to play, not to sing,
Not to join in the fairy thing.
And I stooped like a hawk on the wing
To snatch at the prey I needed!
And oh I have cheated the fairies
And stolen the fairy thing!

Ann: Oh Kate . . . I can speak with my own voice . . .

Kate: My dear.

Ann:
Kate!
It is off, it's away,
The thing I hate!
Oh joy, oh bright day,
Sweet sun, clear air!
I was so long in there,
So long inside,
So long, as if I had died
And been buried under earth.
Now I can laugh and say
Oh gay, oh mirth!
Good-bye, thing I hate,
Gone for ever away,
And thanks, and thanks to Kate,
My darling Kate, my dear
Sister without blame or fear,
My sister Kate!

(They kiss one another. Enter the Well Prince.)

Kate:

>The spell is off my sister Ann
>And here she stands so bonny.
>Come and kiss her if you can,
>Sweet as bread and honey!

Well Prince:

>If I have dreamt, the dream's come true,
>Girl of roses and honey dew!
>Ann, oh Ann, may I be your husband,
>I the watcher and lover of you?

Ann:

>Prince, oh Prince, it was my dream too!
>Though I was dumb, yet I was true,
>I will be wife if you'll be husband,
>I the watcher and lover of you.

(They take hands and kiss. Enter the Porter.)

Porter: Why, here's our beggar maid back again, and—lawkamercyme, what's come to the little dumb thing?

Well Prince: She has come back to herself.

Porter: Well, well, well, as sure as my name's Peter, such a thing has never happened since I was a little boy-porter! I have the peck of gold measured out and ready for you, Mistress Clever.

Kate: If I am to watch a third night, to watch another night against the fairies, I must have a better reward yet at the end of it.

Porter: Now, what might that be?

Kate: I must have the Sick Prince to marry me.

Porter: There's askings indeed!

Kate: Yet that's what I must have.

Ann: Sister Kate, what will the Sick Prince say to that?

Kate: I do not know. Yes, I do know.

(She hides her face in her hands.)

Well Prince:
Kate, oh Kate, you shall have your will,
If you will stay and watch him still.
You shall have my brother for your own lover
If you bring him safe from the Fairy Hill.

(The Prince and Ann go out one way, the Porter another, shaking his head dubiously.)

Kate:
I will go back,
Back to the angry fairies,
Down the long hazel track
Under the quivering moon.
Oh hands, come help me again,

Cling to the horse's back,
Cling fast through wind and rain,
Ears, be deaf to the tune!
Oh eyes, be quick to see,
Heart, head, to dare,
If the fairies find it is me,
Kate, the stealer!
Yet Kate will never care
Though the fairies should blind the healer,
Magic the double dealer,
Kill Kate the stealer—
If only the Prince will care . . .

ACT IV

SCENE I

The Fairy Hill as before. The Fairies dancing

Fairies (singing):
    The stars hang pale above the wood,
    They wheel and dip and lo, are gone,
    The morning comes to swallow them,
    But we dance on, but we dance on.
    Up and under, in and under,
    Down and under, well or ill,
    He'll go the way he shouldna' go
    And find himself in the Fairy Hill!

Beyond the Hill, above the turf,
In moonlit airs we hang our lure,
And he who once has come to it
Away from us shall find no cure.
Up and under, in and under,
Down and under, well or ill,
He'll go the way he shouldna' go
And find himself in the Fairy Hill!

(Enter the Sick Prince with Kate immediately behind him. Kate hides rapidly, but the Prince sweeps into the dance with the Fairies.)

Fairies (singing):
For he who hears the luring song
Shall get the gifts the fairies keep,
And first shall know the fairy love
And last shall know the fairy sleep.
Up and under, in and under,
Down and under, well or ill,
He'll go the way he shouldna' go
And find himself in the Fairy Hill!

(The Prince breaks away from the dancing, and cries out, anxious and disturbed.)

Sick Prince:
Fairies, stop your song,
Aye, stop your stepping and glancing,
Put a check to all the dancing!

Something is happening wrong,
The dancing should be gayer,
Yes, gayer and stranger.
I am becoming a sayer,
A see-er of danger,
Of danger to the Hill . . .
Fairies, be still, be still,
Listen for danger!

(*For a moment they all stay quiet, lifting their heads
and listening. Kate stays pressed back into the curtains,
mousy still. Then the Fairies grow tired of listening.*)

Fairy (petulantly):
I hear no danger, none,
Nothing to spoil our dance
Till the foolish day's begun,
Till the rising of the sun!
There comes no evil chance
Within the Fairy Hill.
We have stayed too long still,
Fairies!
On with the dance!

(*The Fairies and the Prince dance out on a gust of
music, the quicker second half of the tune. It sounds faintly
from behind. After a time Kate steps out from behind the
curtain, holding up her apron full of nuts with one hand.*)

Kate: They're uneasy now, the fairy folk. Supposing
they came back . . . and looked . . . and found me. What

would they do, the cruel fairy people? Their eyes are side-long and they have little stone knives . . . Oh Prince, I'd bear it for you! Yet it might be you helping them . . . Ah, they're back!

(She hides quickly as the two Fairy women come in, one carrying the Fairy baby.)

Fairy Woman: We'll leave my Star-cap here awhile, Gossip, while we are off to the brew-house making of speedwell wine. Where is a toy for him?

(She puts him on the ground.)

Other Fairy: Why, did he lose the wand, Gossip? Thy Star-cap's a bad bold babe! But we shall find it again in time. Nothing gets far lost in the Hill. See, here's a fine cake for thee, Star-cap, all speckled and spangled like the stars themselves.

(She takes a cake out of the breast of her dress and gives it to the Fairy baby.)

Fairy Woman: That is a fine cake of thy baking! What virtue has it, Gossip, for I know well it has some?

Other Fairy: Now, I'll tell thee. Three bites of that cake and the luring would be off the Prince, he would never come again to the Hill, and all the mortals would say he was well and cured! But that can never be.

Fairy Woman: No, for he is dancing, dancing, he will not see Star-cap nor the cake. The Prince will always come back to us.

Other Fairy: Come, Gossip, we must be off to the brew-house, and thou, Star-cap, play with my spangly cake!

(*The two Fairy women go out, leaving the baby playing with the cake. Kate steps out, glancing around her anxiously, and sits herself down on the floor with the baby.*)

Kate: Oh what a pretty cake! What a spangly, speckly cake! Thou art the one who loves nuts, art not, Star-cap?

(*She takes nuts out of her apron and begins to roll them on the floor.*)

See, Star-cap, all the nuts in the mortal world! Better than a cake, better than a silly cake. See, Kate will make them roll for thee. There—how they roll and jump! Thou canst have every one, Star-cap, and I shall have thy cake to play my own play with.

(*She rolls the nuts for the baby to pick up. He leaves the cake, which Kate seizes. The baby trots out with the nuts. Kate stands up slowly, the cake in her two hands, on the level of her heart.*)

It is all so simple.
In this fairy cake
Lies packed the whole of my life:
All the things I shall do or say,
All the things I shall think or make.
In this cake lie: being his wife:
Our children . . . asleep . . . at play:
Midnight and dawn and day

For a lovely life-time of years.
In this cake all my hopes and fears.
It is all quite simple.

(*She hides the cake in her dress and listens. The lights
might go down again here, and the Fairy tune sound a little. She speaks again.*)

I will not hear the fairy tune ever again. The fairy
dances will go on, but I shall be safe on mortal ground,
and he will have forgotten. Oh poor fairies, poor fairies! I
am stealing the thing you want most.

(*As the tune grows louder, she hides again, and the
dancers with the Prince in the middle of them stream in.*)

Fairies (singing):
   The dancing that was ours all night
   Must end at last, the song must cease,
   There is no danger threatening,
   We lay us down, we sleep in peace.
   Up and under, in and under,
   Down and under, well or ill,
   You'll go the way you shouldna' go
   And find yourself in the Fairy Hill!

(*The Fairies begin to stretch and yawn and settle for
sleep. The Prince smiles down on them.*)

Sick Prince:
   Some power pulls you down.
   You sleepy fairies,

You cannot laugh or frown,
The dreams begin to muster,
Your eye-lids droop,
Your heads like a ripe cluster
Of brown and golden fruits.
See, I must stoop
To touch you, fairies.

(*He stoops down among them, stroking their nodding heads. One Fairy nestles up against him and speaks.*)

Fairy:
We must go, we must go, with our dreams' long flight,
Leave touch and hearing and taste and sight,
But you'll come back
On the hazel track,
Come back to us surely to-morrow night!

(*The Fairy drops away from him to sleep. He stands above them, speaking slowly and as though he were puzzled.*)

Sick Prince:
Green Hill, Green Hill . . . I think of a long day
When I forget the tune the fairies play,
Forget the piping and forget the dancing,
The quick, small feet about the smooth floor glancing,
The warm, sweet air, the fairy bread and wine,
The things that have been yours and have been mine.
Why should I think of evil days and cold? . . .
I took the fairy lure, keep and hold,

I will come back, I will come back to-morrow!
What else is there in life but pain and sorrow,
The struggle after honour, love and wealth,
The being well as mortal folk count health!
No, not till good is evil, white is black,
Shall I choose this. Fairies, I will come back!
The world has nothing lovelier to show
Than your sweet dance-tune swinging high and low.
Dawn . . . I must say the words that bid me go.

(*He steps clear and lifts his hand commandingly towards the green wall.*)

Open, open, Green Hill, and let the Prince go
   through!

(*He goes out through the curtains, and Kate follows quickly behind him.*)

Kate:
   And his lady him behind!

(*She follows him out and away from the Hill and the sleeping Fairies.*)

SCENE II

The room of the Sick Prince. He is lying asleep on the bed, facing the audience. Kate sits beside him on a stool, watching him. The curtain is drawn across the window and it is dusk in the room.

Kate:

He has slept here all the morning, sleeping so still, so
 still,
Since we came back through the hazels from the dawn-
 grey Fairy Hill.
Oh heart, be good, be quiet, you must wait, you must
 wait, you must wait,
You belong to Kate the watcher, you belong to the
 Prince's Kate.
Will he hate you still when he wakens? Maybe, my
 heart, maybe.
His eyes are held by the fairies, and life he cannot see.
I am life. I am his life. Prince, will you turn, will you
 turn?
I am the flame that kindles, the flame that will not burn,
I am the one you are wanting, oh love, I am she indeed,
If you could but turn from the fairies, back to the thing
 you need!

(The Prince stirs in his sleep.)

Oh hush, oh hush, oh hush, my dear whom the fairies
 blind,
I cannot bear you cruel, and when you sleep you seem
 kind!
Oh hush, oh hush, oh hush, and leave the fairies
 behind.

*(The Prince wakes and speaks in a dreamy voice, not
looking towards Kate.)*

Sick Prince:

I dreamt of you, I dreamt of you,
On owl-soft wings I swept, I flew,
The fairy hill was with me still,
The fairy luring drew and drew . . .

*(He leans up on one elbow, looks round and sees her.
He speaks fiercely.)*

Kate!

So you are here still, you with me, Kate that I hate!
Why have the Green Hill people not taken, not bound
    you,
Put green, thin cords round your neck, a thorn trail all
    round you?
Why have they left you with me, to my strong sorrow
    and pain?
Did you come with me last night? Were you in the Hill
    again?

Kate: Why, I was there, Prince. I am only a watcher. It
was my part. I did not hurt. And the fairies did not hurt
me. You have woken early, Prince. Sleep again. As for me,
I'm hungry with my watching, Beggar girls have hungry
stomachs. But I've food here.

*(She takes the Fairy cake out of her dress and begins to
nibble it, watching him stealthily.)*

Sick Prince:

Greedy and grasping, mortal thing!

Greedy you go to the Hill and hide there!
You cannot see the beauties that bide there
Nor hear the tune that the fairies sing!

Kate: Maybe, Prince, maybe. I heard some strange music. But I am hungry now.

(She plays with the cake. He watches her.)

Still, this is good food. Sleep again, Prince.

Sick Prince (suddenly):
Beer to brew and flour to bake,
Oh if I had but one bite of that cake!

Kate: Why, surely, Prince, I can well spare you a bit of my cake.

(She gives it to him; he takes it and eats it, and half sits up.)

It is good then?

Sick Prince:
Beer to brew and flour to bake,
Oh if I had but two bites of that cake!

Kate: There's half of my cake gone, but never mind.

(She gives it to him; he eats it and sits right up.)

Beggar girls are used to going hungry.

Sick Prince:
Beer to brew and flour to bake,
Oh if I had but three bites of that cake!

Kate: Well, there's the third bite and an end of my cake.

(*She gives it to him.*)

I shall have all the crumbs for myself.

(*As the Sick Prince eats the last mouthful of the fairy cake, he stands up, flinging away the green cover from the bed. Kate sits very quiet, watching intently. He passes his hand across his eyes and speaks low and thickly.*)

Sick Prince: What is it? . . . There was a bad dream I had . . . a binding, twisting dream . . . Is it over?

Kate (softly): It is over, Prince.

(*He goes over to the window and suddenly pulls the curtains wide apart, flooding the room with sunlight.*)

Sick Prince:
It is over, over at last, oh truly, it is over.
I can smell sun on earth, the earth-born fields of clover!
Oh sweet, oh kindly earth, oh laughing, oh
    childbearing,
Earth that I lost for so long, oh true and beautiful
    thing!

(*He turns from the window towards Kate.*)

Oh Kate, oh Kate my darling, my dear, my earthborn
    Kate,
Beggar girl of my heart, why did I sleep and wait?
I will have you with me for good, who were with me for
    so much ill,

I will have you here with me, who saved me alive from
the Hill!

Kate (*standing on her feet*): I will have you, Prince . . . I
am not a beggar girl . . . that's no matter. I won you from
the fairies with my own hands and heart and head!

(*The Prince kneels in front of her, and takes her hand
in his.*)

Sick Prince:

Hand, oh hand of my Kate, fingers and palm that I
   love,
Strong little, brown little hand, without a ring or a
   glove!

(*He lifts his hand and lays it over her heart.*)

Heart, oh heart of my Kate, brave heart that beats for
   me,
You shall have my heart for your twin so long as our
   lives shall be!

(*He stands beside her, holding her head between his
hands.*)

Head, oh head of my Kate, forehead and lips and eyes,

Be wise for me now as you have been, be calm and
merry and wise!

(*Enter the Well Prince and Ann, hand in hand.*)

Ann: Oh look . . . oh look . . . she has healed your brother too. We are all healed!

Well Prince: He is healed. Oh Kate, Kate, Kate, we are all healed!

Sick Prince: We are all healed . . .

(They all take hands.)

Kate:

> The lost thing has been found, and the broken thing
> mended,
> On plain and mortal ground, the tale has well ended.
> The fairy lure is broken, the fairy singing is done,
> And the kind word is spoken at the rising of the sun!

CURTAIN

ADVENTURE IN THE DEBATEABLE LAND

"Where am I going?" "To the Debateable Land." But who said it? What was I doing in this taxi with all these odd pieces of luggage, and what, anyhow, was the Debateable Land? I looked into the clock face to see how much it had ticked up and judge by that how far I had come—what station was it? But all I saw on the clock face was a notice in black and red which ticked over from line to line saying:

"In the Debateable Land
That lies between here and Fairy Land
You and I may stray, all day, hand in hand,
If we clearly understand
Well to mark the road we came by,
To know well
Trees that bend and alter, stones we put our name by.
Then we may dwell
Once more, on the kindly shore, on Middle Earth.
But the easiest, quickest way
From the Debateable Land
Is the way to Fairy Land and little Hell."

Awkward, very, and what was I going to the Debateable Land for? "To rescue her, idiot!" At last I identified the voice with this greyish frog-like creature in the corner of the seat, a very old frog which had lost its colour and had a little round Victorian beard under its chin. I remembered suddenly that she was imprisoned here in a small room at the very top of the Tower waiting for the horn to be blown. "I thought only princes did that," I said stupidly.

"Not nowadays," said the creature, "get out!" The taxi stopped with a jerk and I collected the things, armsful of things, and slid out. It was quite an ordinary street with villas in small gardens at each side; just here there was an opening between two of them, a passage, yes, probably leading to a park. Of course a park! And just as I thought that a nurse came out pushing a pram. The only difficulty was that the baby seemed to be lightly covered with green fur like mould. Looking in my purse I found nothing but leaves, round leaves of autumn yellow. But that was obvious: fairy gold the other way round: clever of me to have thought of it. And I paid.

I began to collect my things, only the essentials of a journey, as I found myself remembering, though what was the shop where I had bought them—? Yes, shoes of swiftness, seven league boots (like galoshes to put on over the top of the others in case of emergency), cloak of invisibility, cap of dazzle—a kind of temporary gorgon's head, the permanent ones being so expensive and sometimes leading to such awkward situations—invincible sword, axe of strength, flask of water and comb to throw behind when pursued by giants, whistle for calling birds or fishes—"What this?" "Magic carpet!" snapped the frog, "in carpet bag"—bridle for taming wild horses mended rather incompetently with string, magic mirror, drops of Water of Life, other drops of Lethe water for Dragon, hope the labels won't come off, putty to put in holes at bottom of sieve when necessary—a filthy parcel and so heavy!—gloves for handling red-hot iron, dwarf-made chains for binding lions ("But shall I need them all?" "Likely as not."), magic rope ladder of princess hair—"What's that?" "In the hat-box? The tarn-helm of course, and only *lent* you, mind." The frog hopped slowly round: "I see you've forgotten the spiked shoes for climbing glassy hills," he said, "left them under the seat, I suppose—you would!" "But I didn't know—" "Who put them there? You. Very well," said the frog, "if you need them they'll take seven years to make."

There were no porters, of course, and anyhow it is better to carry these things oneself when one can. I slung them about me, and walked down the passage way between the brick walls. Looking back I saw the opening towards the road and the backs of the villas with lace curtains and little greenhouses. However, the next time I looked back there was something inherently more probable, the stone hall with carvings of snakes that stirred all round the windows, and very horrid shadows going across them inside, the Fourth Hall of course. However, it was improbable that They would look out yet. I took out my notebook and from now on made careful notes of the way.

A boy came out of a side passage, whistling, with a spotted dog trotting after him. We began to talk; he was obviously the third son, in fact he told me his name was Jack, and when he offered to help me with my things I was delighted. And I've still no idea how he managed to steal the whistle for the birds. I stayed that night in the House in the Wood and I counted my things carefully when I came to leave it. Then I found the gold chains for lions were missing. They said I should have left them with the management and disclaimed all responsibility, and pointed out the notice which, of course, I ought to have seen. None of the other things were obviously valuable except the tarn-helm which lived in the locked hat-box and the wishing ring which I kept firmly on my finger even when I was washing my hands.

It was my fault about the magic mirror; I shouldn't have let the girl in the train handle it, but she was so friendly—we'd shared a packet of chocolate and she'd shown me all her magic things (at least she *said* they were)—and conceivably it *was* only an accident when she dropped it. And I ought to have kept a sharp eye on the five children instead of making them paper boats; they got the comb for throwing behind when pursued. The putty parcel dropped out of its string. I ought to have tied it up better that morning. As for the magic carpet I still don't know whether it was sheer carelessness on my part, or not. Everyone said it was. The same with the bridle. No, I just don't know still.

On the other hand I was getting near the Tower. I was gradu-ally beginning to recognise the people of the Other Side; there was a sort of oddness about them, a feeling that one didn't want to touch them, though if, finally, one did brush against one or even shake hands—for it was no use declaring war!—they actu-ally felt quite all right. The man on the horse seemed perfectly real; he dismounted and walked with me and offered to take my things on his saddle, but I said no. "You're right to say that," he said, "I'm Hoggi. I'm going to rescue Swanhild who was carried off by the trolls. But I've had bad luck too and been delayed." He seemed unhappy, and so young, and he had such jolly armour! He pointed me out my Tower, but the first time I came to the wrong side, so of course there was nothing to be done. However, I saw the room at the top with very narrow windows widening out as slot windows do, into rounds at the top and bottom. It was fairly obvious that if one were pursued one would have to crawl through those rounds, fix one's rope ladder to the iron bar outside before one was more than half way through, and then swarm out onto it. Not very nice. It was to be hoped the ladder was long enough. Hoggi showed me the key-holes half way up and then he explained that one was to take a snapdragon flower and push it in; the flower would fit exactly onto the knob inside and allow one to turn it—he picked a snapdragon from the wall to show me. I said: "It's too small," but he showed me how to hold it up in front of my eye and then it was exactly the right size.

We camped together that night, Hoggi and I, and made a fire and sat up late over it, talking. The end of it was I lent him things to replace his own which had got lost in the same sort of accidents as mine. I lent him sword and axe to kill the giants who were keeping Swanhild and making her catch the lice out of their long hair every evening. I was to have them back in an hour, he hoped, when he came riding by with Swanhild on his way back to the King and Queen, her father and mother. He mounted and trotted off, waving to me. Suddenly he said: "They make me do it!" I did not realise for some time what this meant, not till I had waited half a day. Presumably Hoggi was really a prisoner himself, and I hope he will get rescued some time soon. But it was a bad business for me.

I had to go back some way so as to get to the other side of the Tower, and I was terribly worried about all these things I had lost. The only thing I had gained was a certain amount of experience, and particularly the knowledge that the way to deal with the Debateable Land is to take everything that occurs to one, however irrational and pointless, and deal with it rationally. One then gets it onto one's own side and away from the fairies. Whenever I had neglected that (for instance at the inn where I had lost the bridle in the cupboard in the wall) things had gone wrong. On the other hand, by paying attention to it I had accumulated a number of small objects, shells and envelopes and handkerchiefs (including the red one which I had stolen in the shop when it occurred to me to do so, and which I had walked off with quite easily), as well as the sixpence which I had seen the woman in front of me drop, and which I had deliberately kept for myself, and so on. I did not know what good they would ever do me except to appear normal when one was in the dark Tower or wherever it might be, but still something might come of them. They took up rather a lot of room, so that I still had to carry more things than I liked, and spent most of my time looking after them.

It suddenly occurred to me to wish I could get them insured, and then I felt the unmistakable prick that meant the magic ring had for once woken up and started functioning. I took a step on and walked up the steps out of King's Bench Walk. Of course, I thought I must consult Dick about this. When I got to Chambers he was very busy and neither very surprised (but of course I could not tell how long, by Middle Earth time, I had been away) nor very pleased to see me! I put my things down in his room— not for anyone would I have left them out of sight. The gloves for handling red-hot iron were on the table. I sat in the comer while Dick hunted through papers and various people came in and out, solicitors' clerks, I supposed. It suddenly occurred to me that solicitors' clerks very seldom have six fingers on each hand and these with a slight web between, nor are the irises of their eyes this curious reddish colour. And as this went through my mind one of them picked up the gloves and put them in his pocket, and went out. I jumped up and said "He's got my gloves!" But Dick said "Nonsense!" And after all it obviously was nonsense by Middle Earth standards that a solicitor's clerk should pick up the gloves of a barrister's wife and walk off with them. I said I had been losing my things and wanted them insured; he said I was insured already and asked what it was—jewellery? I said no, I began to explain, but when I began on the Debateable Land he said he must just finish these papers first. The wishing ring pricked me again and I had just time to pick up my things before I found myself sitting beside a road in the Debateable Land and one of these very nasty large birds they have there, about three times as high as oneself, was stepping along towards me. Of course no one minds about the birds, for they are the thinnest possible things, scarcely paper thickness, but even if one pokes a stick through them they look at one unpleasantly. It went by. It seemed to me very awkward if I was going to re-visit Middle Earth in this patchy way, taking so much of the Other Side with me. I was very doubtful whether I had really been there, whether what I had seen had actually been Dick himself and either the Inner Temple or Middle Earth!

Things went on like this, and, as I got nearer the right side of the Tower, that wretched ring began to take me back to Middle Earth whether I really wanted to go there or not. Simply thinking about it seemed to do the trick, and I could hardly help doing that sometimes, especially in the evenings or just waking up in the mornings. Then I used to find myself at home, in the nursery say, in the middle of a game with the children. But after the first few times I began to be rather suspicious of this. The nursery itself. Used the cuckoo out of the cuckoo clock always to have just that expression? Or was I imagining it? And—it wasn't for nothing, surely, that Lois had suggested a dressing-up game and, before I could stop her, picked up and put on my cloak of invisibility—and disappeared. At any rate to me. Avrion and Nurse seemed perfectly able to see her still. At first I had been terribly upset, but then—hadn't she, in disappearing, burst into that high thin giggling that by now I had come to associate with the fairies? Had I, for that matter, any real reason for supposing that it had been actually Lois at all?

And was this really Avrion who had, with that much too innocent look, suddenly eaten the magic apple? After all, if it had been him wouldn't the apple certainly have had some effect? I strongly suspected that the children were really the Other Side, so cleverly disguised that I couldn't tell, and that Nurse was also an imitation, as paper-thin as the birds. I made up my mind that the wishing ring had been got at by the Other Side and that the sooner I got rid of it the better.

One day I noticed that Valentine—or more probably the Other-Side-disguised-as-Valentine—had a blue-beaded cracker ring. I collected my remaining parcels and picked her up—it was extraordinarily difficult to believe it wasn't really her when it felt so like her. I cajoled her cracker ring out of her and put it on, and half took off my own wishing ring, and as I did that I caught my imitation baby watching me in a dreadful and entirely adult way. With the cracker ring firm on my finger and the other slipping off I wished myself back. As I melted off into the Debateable Land again, I felt the soft imitation baby hands pulling and pinching mine, and then I was through, having successfully got rid of the wishing ring and having instead the blue-beaded cracker ring which might ultimately be some use. I also found that the wishing ring, perhaps influenced by the cracker ring or perhaps realising that I had seen through it and mastered it, had put me down in the rose-tangle, only a hundred yards from the right side of the Tower.

It was extremely uncomfortable getting out of the rose-tangle. I didn't dare put on the seven league boots, as, although they would have taken me out of the tangle, they would also have taken me past the Tower, even if I'd only tiptoed in them. I got a good deal scratched, and it was annoying to see the white rabbits sitting in their burrows under the great briar stocks, laughing at me. And then, I was at the Tower.

There were plenty of snapdragons to fit into the key-holes, supposing I could trust Hoggi to have told me the truth about that, but could I? At any rate I picked some and put them in my pocket. The question now was, whether the Guardians were about, looking on at me mockingly from crafty, eyeholed lairs, if, as seemed likely, the white rabbits had warned them. Well, there was no use thinking too much about that. I went up the steps and blew the horn, which made a most disconcertingly loud and unmusical noise, calculated to wake anybody. It would have been nice, at this point, to have had the traditional cloak of invisibility; however, it wasn't any good wishing for that now.

I fitted the snapdragons onto the knobs, very doubtfully. However, they did turn—and the whole thing might simply be a trap! I stepped inside, shut the door after me and listened. So far nothing, only the narrow uncarpeted stone steps going up and round a corner, and from below the somber ticking of a clock. I went up. The staircase made four turns and came to a landing. Opposite me was one of Them sitting at a desk disguised as an aged and frowsty female caretaker in a shawl with a bunch of tickets and a pile of small illustrated guide-books. "Pay here, please," she said, and smiled in the kind of way which might easily have turned very unpleasant indeed: They thought they'd got me nicely. Well, I knew it would be no good attempting to pay with Middle Earth currency, but I had the dropped fairy sixpence still, and handed it over with my sweetest smile back. She couldn't do anything but take it. "An illustrated guide-book?" she said, "or some nice postcards of the torture chamber?" No thanks," I said, lightly—I wasn't going to let her know this was my only valid coin—"I always buy my guide-books on the way *back*." And I walked past her up the next bend of the stair.

On the next landing, which was obviously the important one, there was the usual choice of doors. I couldn't see anything through the key-holes and I was rather afraid that if I hung about the two suits of armour against the opposite wall might begin to walk in my direction. At that moment a mouse came out of the corner and hesitated in the middle of the floor. I had a corn ear in my pocket, collected some time ago and unused. I rubbed off a grain and dropped it and stood quite still. The mouse flickered nearer, picked up the grain and ran under one of the doors. Inside there was a squeal and a girl's voice: "Oh Princess—!" I opened the door and walked in.

It was in its way rather a beautiful room, with a hunting tapestry on all four walls—though I never very much like tapestry, for one can't be sure what there mayn't be behind it. There were oak chests and benches and a large oak table with heavy iron candlesticks at each end and a strip of needlework all along it, at which the Princess and her ladies were working. It would now have been quite simple to rescue the Princess, only, at the moment, presumably, when I had opened the door, the Princess and her ladies, making five in all, had turned into dolls and were all staring at me out of china eyes from the far side of the table. Again it would have been quite simple to rescue them all in a bundle if only they had been reasonable sized dolls, but they weren't; they were very slightly under life-size. So it was imperative to discover which was the Princess. They were all dressed more or less alike in long brocade dresses and little jewelled caps, and each of them had a pendant of precious stones—if they *were* precious—hung round her neck on a fine golden chain. Three had long flaxen hair and two had long raven-dark hair. You might think that the one in the middle was sure to be the Princess; but then, the one furthest on the right had a golden needle, and the one next the middle on the left was sitting on a slightly more elaborate chair. On the other hand, the one furthest to the left had a footstool, while the remaining one had hair a good two inches longer than the others.

I tried speaking to them, but it had no effect. I tried sprinkling them with drops of Water of Life. As the drops touched, each doll gave a wriggle and grin, but then went waxen again. It was all most difficult. Then I heard a rustling at the door; I had barred it, of course, but that was no obstacle to the snake which began wriggling through the key-hole. However, I hit the snake on the head with one of the iron candlesticks; that made a nasty mess, but I was only thankful that the candlesticks had actually turned out solid—at any rate solid in regard to the snake. They might so easily have been cardboard!

The real test for princesses is, of course, the rumpled roseleaf, but I had none with me; besides it was inapplicable to the dolls. It then occurred to me that the fault might be in my own method of vision. Unfortunately I had lost the magic spectacles—I always do manage to lose my spectacles, there's nothing odd about that. The only thing to do was to put on the tarn-helm and hope for the best. It would certainly turn me into someone else, presumably with a different kind of vision and perhaps a better one for distinguishing princesses. I took it out of the hat-box and put it on. It was heavy and rather large for me; I suppose it had originally been made to fit young Germans with great mops of shaggy curls, like Siegfried. I also found it a little difficult to breathe in at first, but the moment I looked at those dolls I became quite certain which one I wanted: the left-hand of all. So I picked her up.

It is very curious being someone else, even when one knows one is, as one does when wearing the tarn-helm. All sorts of things are slightly different, to which one is normally so accustomed that one doesn't notice them in oneself. For instance the rhythm of breathing, and the whole muscular tone of the body, not only in movement, but even in rest—including the muscles of the face and body wall—is altered. And if, for instance, one picks something up, the business of gripping and lifting and balancing—although one is doing it as simply and automatically as ever—is a complete surprise. I had no idea of who I was, but I threw the heavy princess-doll over one shoulder (normally I should have tucked her under my arm) and walked out of the room.

As I passed the old imitation caretaker again, I picked up one of the catalogues saying cheerfully "Thanks," and not paying. Then off down the stairs again. Going quickly round a corner I very nearly ran into two of the Other Side waiting quite quietly with a cage for me to walk into. There was nothing for it, then, but to jump out of the window, which was at least fifteen feet from the ground. Ordinarily I shouldn't have landed without a sprained ankle at best, but this other person I had become was fortunately much more athletic than I am and landed without any damage except for breaking the bottle of Lethe water. The stuff inside it smelt disgusting and I noticed that the grass which it splashed withered and turned black under my eyes.

It was obvious that the Other Side would be after me, so I put on the seven league boots (the ordinary shoes of swiftness had never been much use since being cleaned with fairy shoe-polish) and set off for Warning Crag, the most obvious landmark in the Debateable Land. It is not so easy as you would suppose, walking with seven league boots, as one can't see where one's next step will take one—very likely into a ditch or a bramble bush; it is quite hopeless to try to run in them and really one has to deliberate over every step. I knew, naturally, that the dragon's nest was somewhere near Warning Crag, but the creature was usually asleep and I hoped to get by safely. However, as luck would have it, my seven league boots landed me right on the dragon's tail and the wretched thing woke up and began snorting fire at me. I hadn't got the Lethe water for it, but I threw it the stolen hand-kerchief, telling it to blow its nose, and it was so surprised that it stopped long enough for me to take another step on and out of its nasty, smelly nest.

After this it was all fairly plain sailing. Once I did miss my way rather badly, and several times I had to evade the Other Side by one stratagem or another. I never let go of the doll-princess, though I found her a great nuisance and became less and less ceremonious in the way I handled her. I kept on the tarn-helm the whole time and stayed as the person I had become, which gave me great physical advantages; I never discovered who the other person was, though often I found myself remembering things and people which are no part of my own memories. There are moments when I think she must have been a gym or games mistress at some school; some of the visual memories which I had were certainly not English, but might have been, say, American.

And then I came to the brick-walled passage leading out of the park past the villas. I walked along it, whistling (a thing I never do myself) and there I was in the street I had started from. And there was the frog. The frog said to me: "So you didn't get the Princess after all! You are a fool, aren't you?" "But—" I said, and looked round, for I knew I had hold of the doll. Then I saw that the doll had her feet on the ground, that the doll was definitely holding onto me, and that she had grown to life-size. "Aren't you the Princess?" I asked the doll. The frog, of course, answered. "No, she isn't—where are your eyes? Proper fool you'll look, taking *that* back to the palace!"

"But—" I said again.

Then the doll said, in a most un-princesslike voice: "I'm Joan. That's all. But don't worry. That nasty stuck-up little Princess wouldn't want to get rescued by you—I know her! She said she wasn't going to let anyone under a prince with ten thousand a year rescue her, and there's sure to be one soon."

"But—" I said.

"I didn't *ask* you to rescue me, did I?" said Joan, in rather a hurt, proud kind of voice, and stepped back, letting go my arm. When she did that I noticed that her long brocade dress shortened and smoothed out into a printed cotton and her long hair rolled itself up under the beret which the little jewelled cap had turned into. She added: "If you hadn't rescued me, no one would have. Girls like me don't get princes to rescue them."

The frog croaked: "Listen to her, the hussy! And you ought to have rescued the Princess, you know you ought. You were told to."

"Who told me, anyway?" I asked. I was rather cross.

"Well, I told you, for one!" said the frog; "and now, suppose you take off that tarn-helm and give it me back. Lost most of the rest, haven't you, proper fool—"

"You shut up!" I said, and I took off the tarn-helm and dropped it on the frog. It clanged on the pavement and disappeared, and so did the frog. I only hope he took it back to wherever it belongs. At the same moment a taxi drew up and I knew I had to be getting along back to Middle Earth. "Can't I give you a lift, Joan?" I said. "I'm awfully glad it was you, not the Princess!"

Joan said: "I know you now, with that silly old hat off. I've got to get off to work—I'm a mill-hand on Middle Earth—but we'll meet again. I did find out that much in the Tower."

"When?" I asked, one foot on the step of the taxi.

"First of May, I think," she said.

"But what year?"

"Well, it ought to be next, by rights," she said, "but you never know, the way time gets messed about these days. Well, so long and thank you."

"Till then—" I called after her as the taxi started, and the lines of the notice began ticking over on the clock face:

"In the Debateable Land

That lies between here and Fairy Land . . . ."

MAIRI MACLEAN AND THE FAIRY MAN

I

Oh maybe 'tis my rock
And maybe 'tis my reel,
And whiles it is the cradle
And whiles it is the creel.

I should be redding my house,
But oh, I'm stepping away
To hear high up in the fern
The tune that the fairies play.

Oh my bonny stone house
With the meal ark full to the brim!
But my fairy man's in the fern
And I must away to him.

And it's Mairi, Mairi MacLean,
Ach, Mairi MacLean, come ben!
But I am stepping away
Adown to the hazelly glen.

Oh folks may look upon Jura,
And he may be rich who can,

But all the Isles of the Sea
Are for me and my fairy man!

Oh I've made songs at the shearing
Till the tears and the laughter ran,
But a bonnier song than mine
Is sung by my fairy man!

Oh I was milking my ewes,
And it tinkled fine in the can,
But all the flocks in the world
Are for me and my fairy man!

Oh I was weaving a plaid,
And asking myself for whom?
When I spied my fairy man
And I left the clicketting loom.

And maybe 'tis my bairn
Who cries her dinner is slow,
But she sees her mammy's in love
So she lets her mammy go!

And maybe 'tis my rock
And maybe 'tis my reel,
And times it is the heckling combs
And times it is the wheel . . .

II

Scarba is purple glass; the ruffling waves grow dim.
Wild deer of Scarba, swim to me over the sound,
Ach, Corryvrechan pulls you, but swim to me strongly,
    swim!
There is no stag of you all that runs as lightly as him,
Stepping on my quick shadow, pinning it to the ground.

Luing is low on the sea, a dark and a gentle land.
Blackbirds of Luing, rise high in your airy throngs,
From the tall red fuchsias of Luing, fly low, fly across to
    my hand!
Blackbirds, hark to his singing, for well you should
    understand
The way that a grown woman gets caught in a net of songs.

All night the Paps of Jura are standing against the stars.
Oh paps of the Jura Woman that dreams of her lover's
    breast!
My breasts are remembering Uistean across all fairy bars;
Though I, too, am a mother, freckled with suckling scars,
Yet I would that his head were lying here on my heart's
    nest.

III

Though you should bid me keep still, keep still,
And set my body to yours in kindness,

Though I should smile in a magicked blindness
On hands that strangle and eyes that kill,
Though for your sake I turn thoughtless, mindless,
You shall not possess me, nor no man will:
For I am the woman who writes the songs
So I cannot stay in the Fairy Hill.

IV

Oh wha's this couching at my breist bane?
Is it a sick bairn or a foul black stane,
Or naught but my ain fetch weeping by her lee-lane?

Oh my puir fetch-thing, weep not sae sair!
He is far in his ain place, he will come nae mair,
Not in the gowany glen nor along the wave edge bare.

Stand up, thou Self of me, for we maun come to grips!
We will forget the fairy and the light that doonses and
    dips,
And the eyes and the hands of him, and the brushing of
    his lips.

V

Oh maybe 'tis my rock
And maybe 'tis my reel,
And whiles it is the cradle
And whiles it is the creel.

Oh maybe 'tis the meal ark
That stands beside the wall,
And maybe 'tis the weaving,
And I'll be seeing to all.

And maybe 'tis the pot,
And maybe 'tis the pan,
But I can write songs as good
As the songs of the fairy man!

THE LITTLE MERMAIDEN

It never does any good, no, never, never. I too remember Dafnia;
I too remember the things that happened to her. She! She was
always soft and silly, mooning about by the edges. What business
has a mermaid to be like that? Any of us like to climb out on to a
rock now and then, to get that lovely, dangerous sense of evanes-
cence when the film begins to dry off one in the sun and one's
skin tingles to the air; all of us like to lie out on a yellow beach
and feel the hot sand wriggle and tickle in under one's scales—
when one knows that in a moment one can be plunging back into
the clean water. All of us like playing among the weed tangle,
rocked in the slippery, purple-brown cradle, parting it with hands
and tail. And then there's coming to an estuary, or better, where
some quite little stream drops down through rocks and in, where
the sweet, flower-tainted water is seized on and ducked and held
under by the waves breaking onto its flow, till it gives way and
mixes and is taken, it and all its earth-things, its straws and
branches and fir-cones, its smell of man and cattle and land-
birds. But one can have enough of edges. And then it's out and
down, to the deep rhythms, the dark quiet of our own which is so
good, so far better than all the crashing and bursting, the flying
foam, the angry hollows and retreats of edges. Better above all
than shallows and compromise, low-tide pools, places of nets and
stakes. For after all, when one has said everything, it yet remains
that edges mean man.

But she—it was as though something were wrong deep inside her, something that made her different, even at the beginning, from the rest of us mermaids. It was always edges for her, and warmth and softness; the only game she played was the quicksands game. She would swim with the ships by moonlight; well, we've all done that in our time, but Dafnia never kept her distance, she seemed to forget the chances of their soiling her, she seemed almost to enjoy the smell of cooking and harbours and tarry feet. We warned her, and when we understood that she wouldn't listen to us, we took her to the Queen, our hands bearing on her angry, slippery shoulders, down, down to the still, untainted, deeply salt water and the Green Palace. We left her alone with Queen Thetis and not one of us asked her what was said. But after that she was sulky and not to be spoken to for weeks; she would sit on the bottom with her hair tangled and heavy, and if anything passed her she would hit out at it, snatching the crabs' legs off or grinding stones into the poor soft anemones; even the jelly-fish grew frightened of her and wavered away when they felt her coming. She would only speak to the sea-gulls, and we all know what kinds of shore-tales they have to tell!

And then the storm came, and the rest of us thought we must make it up with Dafnia and get her to come and play the storm-games. We were all tingling and thrilled with it, our strong tails were straightening and threshing among the bursting bubbles, our hair was piled with foam. We went hurrahing through the crests and Dafnia along with us, and we thought now she had become a true mermaid again.

When we came up with the boat, she was already half over, her sail wet and hindering. We went salmon-dancing all round her, laughing at the gilding on prow and strakes, laughing at the wet men, loosening the little courage they had left. We did not notice Dafnia then nor catch her looking in any special way—as we know now she must have done—at the young man in the drenched pale shirt and velvet coat and hair as dark and glistening as a conger's back. The boat went over and filled with the eager breaking water, and glad waves slapped the drowning mouths, and all was to be clean and mixed again and part of the long story of Thetis. We wanted that.

And then we saw that Dafnia had hold of the man, touching him not yet dead. We have all touched them when they are dead, the dreadful leaping heat washed out of them. When they are beautiful we use them for a time to deck out the halls of the Green Palace. We have stripped the sodden canvas from the bodies of sailors, the silk and linen from the bodies of those who paid money to be taken in ships, we have draped their white fluent limbs over knots of coral and hung them by their heels from the under-sea cliffs to wave arms no longer hot and hostile and mix their land hair with the long ripple of the weeds. That is one thing, but to touch them alive and uncooled, as Dafnia was doing—ah, we cried to her to drop it, at first angry and shocked, then desperate for her own safety. Some of us tried to snatch it away, but we could not bring ourselves to touch it. But she kept hold of it, kept its face above water, her hands under its shoulder, the flukes of her tail holding up its trailing legs. And her face was set and quiet and stupid looking, as though a net were dragging her, although it was she herself who was her own net.

We could not bear it; we dropped away and watched her take it to an island, pushing it up onto rock after rock, higher out of reach, and so to grass and sea-pinks. We saw it begin to move, sit up and become irrevocably a man. And at that we dived down, clamouring, the steep waters pressing clean on our eyeballs, to tell our Queen of what had befallen our sister.

The next day Dafnia came back to us, but none of us could touch her hand now or ask her to join in our games. Nor did it seem as though she wanted that. But in a day or two we had begun to forget; the thing we had seen was rocking away from us with every hour of the long swells that had followed the storm. We were planning a moonlight porpoise hunt, and she was with us again. Then suddenly she said: "On the land there is hunting of four-legged deer with horns like fine coral, only brown and stronger. They ride on horses, with their legs branching on each side of the horse's back." That was very horrible; for a moment none of us could speak to answer her. She went on and she was not looking at us: "On the land they dance on grass and in palaces; their legs bend and lift and toss in the air. The women wear shoes of all colours on their feet; when a man is a prince men bend down and kiss his feet, and when a woman is loved by a prince, it may be that her feet are kissed by him."

We heard her out. And we shivered as one does in a cold current with one's upper part, and we felt as one does when the shark catches some smaller fish, and one is not near enough to save it. The things she said grated like sharp gravel on our scales. And then she spoke again: "He has gone home to the land and his palace and I must follow him."

So then with a great effort and wavering of flukes I forced myself towards her, to take her hand. I said: "You cannot, Dafnia.

Edges may be one thing; but this is beyond edges, beyond the tops of beaches. Think what that means, Dafnia—it will be dry!" And she said: "It was dry on the island in the hollow the spray did not reach; the sea-pinks were dry and thin."

I saw then that in her other hand she held some crushed wet heads of sea-pinks. I said: "Forget the sea-pinks and all this. You must. If you do not you cannot be one of us mermaids ever any more." And we all trembled when I said that terrible thing to Dafnia, and I remembered how she had struggled awkwardly and uglily up over the rocks of the island, pushing and lifting that—man.

But, if she heard at all, she did not heed. Her hand was slack as low-tide weed in my hand. She said: "Sisters, I am going to the witch."

I dropped her hand then; I could only say: "Why?" very low, but I knew or half knew the answer she was bound to make.

"I am going on land," she said. "I am going to walk on feet."

We drew away from her then; there was nothing more to say; we saw her float from among us until she hung, little and shining-pale, suspent over the great hole above the waving of tentacles. She knotted up her hair and straightened herself; she lifted her hands and clasped them over her head, and dropped through the little space between the tentacles and was lost.

There were none of us by her in her wanderings below; she had chosen to be alone; she could not be recalled to wishing otherwise. But those with tentacles had overheard and whispered by moonlight to the mackerel, and the mackerel told the thing to us. Dafnia had sat for a long time in silence by the cave, on the stone, until the witch knew what was in her heart. And then the witch had sheared Dafnia's hair with a sharp pearl shell, and with the same shell had slit and carved and divided her, making her human-shaped. And with the human feet and legs, Dafnia had also taken on human mortality. She would become the thing that men become after drowning and before the fish have cleaned and whitened their bones into cool permanence. Yet, even so, she could not become wholly human, she could not have whatever this thing is which they claim is better for them than our calm sea-living for all time, this violence more than storms, this brightness more than sunshine, this clinging-together more than touched limpet to rock, this troubled thing which humans call the soul. I cannot tell why they, who are shaped like us in their upper parts, yet never perfect, should yet be different, nor whether this soul of theirs makes up to them for their lack of bodily perfection. It is better not to think of them, to stay in our own world, mixed and flowing with it for ever.

But the mackerel told us that the witch had made it plain to Dafnia that she might not have this human thing called soul unless she herself were to become mixed with the human, the prince, as before she had been mixed with us and the sea, and this would only come to be if the prince were to love her. "She has made a bad bargain," said the silvery flipping mackerel, "for she will not get her soul without the prince's love—think of it, mermaids, mixing with a human! She has lost her hair and she is blemished as a body, and now when she walks on her new feet, it hurts her as though she were walking on sharp shells." And they told us how the witch had sent her, now that she was no longer a mermaid, through the twisting, dry way, under the rocks of the very bottom, and so up onto land.

So she was lost to us; it was no use remembering her. In storm or calm we did not think of her. We would sweep south with the whales into the sticky, tingling water which fills our warm hair with sparkles, where soft flashes gleam along our slowly plunging bodies. Or we would turn and head north pouring along the tepid currents until we came to the iceberg seas, deep diving down their under cliffs and into their tinkling inner caves and clefts. And one day we came back to the beaches of the land where Dafnia had gone, and it was just before dawn.

As we were playing there among the light surf, we saw a woman coming down the cliff path, wearing the thick woollen skirt and kirtle of land folk, stuff that smells half of sheep and half human. She had no basket or burden on head or hips, as most women have, nor had she nets piled on her arms. And she walked waveringly, as though each step were pain. Hiding in troughs and hollows, sea and sand coloured, we watched her come down to the beach and strip off her heavy clothes; her hair was between short and long, and partly grey. Her body seemed soft and blemished as land women's bodies are, because they must wear woollen clothes and carry burdens, and because their souls tear through the flesh and skin. Yet it was not altogether a land woman's body; and a thought came to me, and I cried out "Dafnia!" and she held her arms out and ran unevenly forward into the first of the little waves.

We all came round her then, but not touching her, for she was tainted. And I said: "Have you found your human soul, Dafnia?"

And she cried out in a soft bleating voice: "No, for he never loved me, he would not let me mix with him!"

"What, then?" I asked.

And she said: "It is all over. The land does not want me."

Then I: "You cannot come back, Dafnia. You cannot be a mermaid any more, nor can the things that the witch has done ever be undone."

She looked at me with her eyes that had become half human and said: "Oh, are you sorry for me?" And her mouth went soft and shapeless and tears began to go down her cheeks.

It seemed to us strange and horrible that Dafnia, who had been a mermaid, should say and do that; it seemed so strange that we all laughed. And then an even stranger thing happened. For Dafnia went on into the sea, deeper and deeper, stepping with her woman's feet, and we thought she was going to drown as humans do. But instead, the waves washing against her were wearing her away as though she had been made of sand, a sand pillar. The sun was rising now and the edges of the waves were crinkled gold and flesh colour with the light beating through them, and all this colour was dashing and breaking on Dafnia, and all the time she was becoming shapeless, blotting out, no more than the first pattern of something that could have become either woman or mermaid. And in another minute, as the sun rose fully, even that shapelessness became worn away. Where Dafnia had been there was nothing now but dancing waves and foam, and perhaps a mixing again with us mermaids and the sea world which is ours.

PAUSE IN THE CORRIDA

Black bulls of hate, charging across the mind,
You are met, are stopped here.
Not by red cloaks, colour I most love and hate,
But by green, colour of fields and certainty,
Blue, colour of sky and time,
White, colour of sleep, no colour.

At mid-age, sick and suddenly,
I found myself in the thick of a dark wood.
How lost, paths I once knew were right!

Black bulls, small bulls, quivering with life and anger
Against the smell of death certain, death only minutes ahead,
Here is a pasture for you, here: here, see
Green grass not lost for ever:
Green grass to lie on.
The smell of cider apples,
Music in the ears, flowers,
Books and a great wood fire, rest and dignity,
Pattern and reason through all.

Rest, my bulls, rest.
And while the bulls rest, you, dear friend, dear comrade,
(Calling you comrade in my thoughts, I shall not wake
Frowns and distress) you, who have been here

Before the time of the bulls, you, who thought of me then
    kindly,
Think of me kindly still. For I am in need of kindness
Because of the bulls. As the bulls also are
In need of kindness.

Rest in the pastures, bulls, and perhaps, next time
You will get the picador and the matador.
In spite of the cleverness and the flapping cloaks and the paper-
    bright barbs,
You will get them down.

But the bulls say, supposing we never want to leave these
    pastures?
They will be green and quiet for ever.
There will be water in summer,
There will be sleek cows for us,
The gad-flies are gone for ever,
We will be quiet for ever.

The pear tree has been growing for a hundred years.
The walnut tree has been growing through ten generations of
    mankind.
On the south side of the house there are green grapes.
Will that suffice us?

The Normandy girls in the kitchen never bother their heads.
It is a pity the white horse has colic, but let us remember
He was getting old.

The lovers have gone for a short walk.
The brother is playing Schubert.
The father is reading a grave book.
Will that suffice us?

The stones of the house are strong.
The thatch holds firm on the cottages.
Afforestation is regular.
At the inn the peasants are drinking cider.
Will that suffice us?

I slept ten hours last night.
If I sleep late I often have bad dreams.
This morning, then,
Dozing, I saw a hideous and malignant face—
Knew I was in for a nightmare—
Tried to bolt—knew it could catch me—began to put
In gear all mechanisms of fear and horror—
And then—
Almost at the moment of contact, I turned and said:
Are you for the revolution too, comrade?
And, as it caught me,
As, in a nightmare, the supreme moment of horror ought to
  have come,
The face, although still ugly,
Had ceased being malignant, had become
The face of a friend.
And, as he kissed me kindly,
I awoke and it was a warm morning and I could smell

Coffee and fruit.

Was that a dream, a delusion,
Was it, was it?
Can there be a change of heart?
Or must for ever
The hundred year old pear tree blossom and bear and ripen
    fruit,
And the grapes ripen on the manor house,
And the old ideas blossom and ripen in men's minds,
Ripen and rot? And rot.
And the bulls rot in the beautiful pastures.

Black bulls, black bulls, the corrida is still on.
We have got to go back,
Go back and die.

BRÜNNHILDE'S JOURNEY DOWN THE RHINE

Flames now of soft darkness were at wave lap round me, tongued and overwhelming darkness; the movement of this darkness woke me from aloof dreams into following it, into a long statement of shapes. Through the edges of shapes appeared stars, far and familiar. Between stars, crescent moon, quiet, rideable. But why think thus? Grane, I said, my horse, my horse, you and I will be careful of one another and there will be no need of other wings. Yet came no nuzzling Grane to my hand outreached for contact. What then? My spread of fingers encountered neither rock nor thin mountain blossom. This smoothness was planed pinewood, and what behind, what knockings, what chick to break this plank-egg? Ah, I thought, no chick, flimsy and single, but a moving of all unbroken onward together, ripple-beating of mountain-flow. I am, thought I, in a boat and this, yes, at my back, hard narrowness of boat strakes between me and river. Shifting my eyes sideways from stars, on either side almost fire-shaped, yet thick, yet static, peaks jagged: my dark flames hardened to rock by cold Rhine-stream. Shapes changed with downward drifting slowly; capes blocked out oblongs or coarse triangles of stars; valleys were sharp cups; ranges gently unfolded; night held.

At dawn I raised myself, remembering, and looked. In front of me was the man Gunther, unshaven, with tongue flickering over lips and eyelids over eyes. Could it then have been he who broke the flame-ring, he the fearless and wise? Fearless, I thought, fearless, what does that mean? And now—oh now what was this in myself, this shrinking and shivering, this softness of muscle fibres avoiding bruising, this loathly acceptance by eagerly pretending flesh and spirit of something hideous and hated? Let me consider, I cried to myself, give me at least a moment to consider, what is this new thing that has befallen me? It must be, myself whispered back, that this is fear, this is what makes nidderings shriek and vomit and caper laughably in the moment before the seen spear enters. It is as All-Father said, I should know the mortal things, of which this is one. I am sorry now that I and my sisters laughed so often at the death of nidderings. And this sorriness is again mortal, it is pity, it is the thing that comes to mortal women between battles in hall and bower, and they are got with child and trouble by men whom they should better have laughed at. Thus has All-Father dealt with me. And I regarded Gunther and the other men, with a dry mouth and hands too cramped to hit.

What did I fear? Not surely their swords which I saw all the time were ill-made and easily blunted. Not their spears, unbalanced and with bad grips. Not their foolish banner scribbled with ravens. But what? Was it their possessing hands, eyes, breathing and hotly wriggling bodies, ready to melt over me and smother me like wax suddenly dripping on a brittle fly? The man called Gunther moved his hands about on his thighs, on the coarse woollen cloth itchy above the skin. "So," he said, digging at me with his eyes; and the envious digging eyes of his men slid and flickered between him and me.

"So"—? I thought—but no! How is this? The man Gunther is not brave or his men would not be envious, would not be thinking against him and over him instead of for him and through him. Nor is he wise, for were he wise he would be speaking to me, not digging at me with his eyes as a greedy man digs pudding with a horn spoon. Yes, he would be speaking to me and then my mind would awake outwardly and I would not still suffer dark flames wavering through me bursting into light fringes at brain level. But he is not speaking to me because he does not want to, he does not know or care whether I stand firm on ground, or rock in All-Father's flames. He does not want speech with the woman who I am, but rather possession of the woman whom he thinks he sees and whom he thinks will be made his by continuous sight and grasp and hearing, by the constant usage of her mouth and lips for smell and taste. That is neither courage nor wisdom. What, has All-Father played tricks on me, his wish-child? Or is it that some new invention or corruption has come between the Norns and their spinning, something put in from outside, some accident? Ha then, I said, upright on the thwart, why stay? Grane, my horse, my horse, come to me, let us leap!

But again no Grane came, no whinny from the boat, no hoof-stamp on by-gliding beach or rock or thicket. Only a giggle from the ripple at the prow and the prancing dive of Flosshilde or Woglinde and their weialala lifting and cradling the boat down the long, sweeping, water-smooth plane of the Rhine-slope. Sisters, ah sisters, I whispered at them past the thick crouching me-ward-looking men, Woglinde, Flosshilde, Wellgunde, where, where is Grane my horse? And they answered, tossing in light bubbles, "The horse has gone to the hero. Siegfried has Grane."

In the three rings of their diving leialala the name echoed growing as the ripples lessened. No trick of All-Father, but Siegfried the brave and wise who had parted the flames and come to me, young and certain: Siegfried who comes always the straight way fearless, as the birds and beasts know, giving him fearlessness back: Siegfried giver and not taker. Somewhere, I said to myself, Siegfried will be, and we shall look at one another straight without hurting fear or digging greed. Then all will be well. Only may it be soon because it is loathsome for me being among these Gibichungs, in their dirt, for them to tread, and with the flames springing up ever and blotting out from moment to moment my purpose of me.

At mid-day they ate, grabbing and belching, and in undertones promising quarrels, hands ever at knife-hilts. Gunther must needs share with me meat and mead, heavy-smelling, an occasion for his gripping paws to slide and fondle. In the heat and sparkle of the afternoon he spread a cloak in the bows and winked me to it. But I was still dazed with flames and currents and remembrance; I did not move. He would not force me in front of his men, even he, even they. And in their hearts all were proud that I did not move, since a wife, in their way of it, should be cold and constantly forced: thus men show their power with their pleasure, not only the Gibichungs but all tribes of men who are not more than mortal.

During the afternoon some slept, and the Rhine daughters out of the surface sparkle threw evil dreams at them, so that they twitched and jabbered and pulled wry faces in their sleep. It seemed that Woglinde and her sisters had lost something, yet what it was I could not tell because of the waving and breaking of the flames between me and them. And in the evening we came to the black rocks and the ravens flying and the heavy pillars of the Gibichung house reflected in the wine-coloured Rhine-stream.

Strange cries and shouts rose ahead of us, blare of war-horns and burst of warning drums, clanging of magic bells to avert evil, since they were afraid of what I might be. As I too was afraid. So in a fear-sunset our boat steered in to the landing-place. Above on the highest rock was Hagen among the ravens, black as the bridal night. Below clustered and swarmed the ragged hosts, savage, suspicious even of their own lice, their own leaders, their own women, loading their bodies with bronze and hides, their heads with horns and feathers stripped from dead forest creatures. From behind, girls peered and peeked, fear-shy, dirty, with matted hair, not knowing themselves as persons, with reason or purpose, but willing to accept all from the men.

In the house of the Gibichungs was light of torches. More girls came out, these with combed hair flower or gold decked, and gold and amber at breast or waist. But they too walked in fear, or with little hard spurts of anger and greed, clustered together lest some wrong man take them; since they were for the man with the most gold on his belt and bracelets, the most spells on his sword and spear, and the most power of death over other men. These girls waved hands and branches, welcoming me, crying to me to become one of like kind with themselves. For me, as for them, would be flesh-feasts, stories and singing and displaying of craft, the showing of themselves fine and well-clad to the men on May Days and Midsummers, the hot flicker of the digging eyes warming their skins to pink. For me, as for them, would be winter coziness in crowded bowers, the woman-smell, the gossip, the giggling retreat from men's hands clutching at skirt or ankle on the stairs at the back of the dais, while outside snow might drift, frost hold, Gods walk the bare woods or treacherous river-ice, bondsmen and bondswomen freeze to chilled submission on straw in huts. For me, as for them, the life of the Gibichungs.

I stood by Gunther on the landing stage in shrunk horror, aware all the time of this new thing, fear, pinching me like new shoes. Is this your will, All-Father, I said, that I am to be turned into this kind of animal? Must I now say good-bye to my own purpose, my own life? The shields clashed horribly in the gathering darkness, and Gunther laid creeping hands on me and spoke of me as a beast of the chase, a champion deer or bear at last shot down by the might and cunning of a Gibichung. And it was as though I were an empty pelt, a dead carcass which could not flee from knife or teeth.

Then through the swan-herd of Gibichung girls, one came thrusting in pride of waist-long yellow hair, much gold, much amber, much coral, proud upward curling of polished bronze, the princess, Gutrune. She was the centre of all that, and she had Siegfried by the hand.

Yet I did not for one moment consider her hand in his. I only knew that after all there was escape. This Gibichung evening was not real, was not to last, was not to catch me. We two should at once get clear of it, into reason and gentleness of our own; and all would be as the Norns had spun for us. All this was so certain that I stepped forward saying, Siegfried! I was thinking of his gladness in escaping with me from the scuttling darkness of fear-stricken greed, from the black flames. Siegfried!

He did not step forward to meet me, glad of an equal at last.
His face was young and merry. He looked at me. He seemed to
know me with his eyes yet not to know me with his blood, as I
knew him. He only knew me as Gunther knew me, as the new
possession of the Gibichungs. Yet did my certainty of him not
waver. These were his hands, his mouth, his body. Yet other. He
had been changed. As he spoke, and as Gunther spoke, and as I
did not speak but waited, I became aware of how much. He was
still brave but he was no longer wise. Reason had gone from him,
and clarity, and the straight way.

Grane, my horse, my horse, that was the end, that had to be
the end, was it not so? He had touched evil things; he had
touched gold and would not share it; he had come to the house of
the Gibichungs and had been taken by it instead of hating it; he
had been willing to change his own shape, the very shape of his
clear mind; he had wanted the flesh-feasts and the boastings of
the women, the power over men and the blood-brotherhood
with Gunther. They had but shown him these things and he had
trusted childishly, and childishly desired the chief prize, Gutrune.
Worse followed bad. He had laughed at the Rhine maidens and
he had forgotten the flames and the cold rock of the mountain
top. Grane, my horse, my horse, how if he was young, innocent,
without knowledge of the Gibichungs and their enchanted cup?
Because of that let him still be held hero, let him be remembered
as he was. Because of that let build the resin-flaring pyre to destroy all that was evil, to burn up, wood with vermin, the Gibichung house, collapse of beams to back-break master with slave.
Let build the pyre to burn the body that was once wise friend of

wood-birds, once queller of flames, once Siegfried. Let build the split-log pyre whose heat shall draw subtly the cold Rhine daughters, up, up, weialala, lap-giggling rock to black rock, then sudden terror of spread, and so to lie finally quiet, current-smoothed over a no longer bubbling ruin, over soaked and dispersing ash that will have been us. Because Siegfried was young and still wise on the mountain top, let build the pyre to wipe out fear with fear and flame with flame until all shall be even as at the first even spinning of the Norns. Let me topple now from the precipice of dark and unbearable flames into the light flames which must for a moment be borne, and then nothing will again be nothing as in the no-time before All-Father wished me into being. Grane, my horse, my horse, because all was once well it makes no difference to the ending.

THE BORDER LOVING

The wan water runs fast between us,
It runs between my love and me,
Since the fairy woman has made him a fairy
And sat her down upon his knee.

Eden Water flows cold between us
And west of Eden the Solway tide,
But the fairy woman she came from Ireland
And my love stayed on the further side;
My love lies snug in Carlisle Castle
With the changeling woman for year-long bride.

Waters of Tweed are deep between us,
Fierce and steep the unridden fells;
But the fairy woman watches the swallows
And tastes the clover and hears the bells,
And my love watches and hears and follows.

MIRK, MIRK NIGHT

(for strange roads, with Zita)

O they rade on, and farther on,
    And they waded rivers abune the knee,
And they saw neither sun nor moon,
    But they heard the roaring of the sea.

It was mirk, mirk night, there was nae starlight,
    They waded thro' red blude to the knee;
For a' the blude that's shed on the earth
    Rins through the springs o' that countrie.

It was during the seventh year that I began to become aware of where I was and why. No sudden or startling event brought these hidden things to consciousness, but rather a succession of small enlightenments. It is perhaps not well known to those on Middle Earth that we others in Fairy Land are not used to look too directly up nor down. Our eyes in downward gazing seldom encounter anything nearer to ground than the thousand clustering tops of fern and flower, ankle-height violet or primrose, and knee-height orchis or burnet rose. The trees, also, bow down to the reaching gaze or grasp, letting drop apple or chestnut candle. To one lying in the thick lee of a hawthorn hedge, there is no sky, but only layer upon layer of spreading and dizzying branches, enclosing hollows full of that scent which is half goat and half utter sweetness, and which is ever to be found in Fairy Land at yet other seasons than May. Nor do the upper windows of the great columned and vaulted halls of Fairy Land look towards anything but the soft sway of boughs and tendrils, and sometimes a flight of birds.

Yet it happened to me once in a ball game with my friends and companions, that one clutched at me laughing, and broke my necklace, which pattered down over my breast and past my knees. He laughed and said we should find another as good in the hall of precious things, but I, a little angry, said I must indeed have again what I had lost. So down I went, groping for my necklace in the thick, flawless, earth-covering grass, and at last I found it. But as I did so, as my fingers touched the beads, so also I touched what was below the grass, and this was hard and smooth. At that it came to me suddenly that nothing could root there, and I was momentarily blinded by a vision of white, twisting, easily broken roots. Carefully parting the grass-blades, I found that it was indeed as I thought. The ground—for it was neither earth nor sand nor rock—was dry, polished, unpierceable. And as I knelt there, the thought came clicking into my mind of my own fingers on another kind of foundation. I remembered first the mossy brittleness of forest banks under my soft baby grabbing, and then, with a certain shock and withdrawal, the wet clay round old cabbage stumps, parting with a reluctant stickiness as the root heaved up, and the rain on my shoulders, and the cabbage-smelling clay blocking my fingernails.

But as I sprang to my feet, breathing hard and clutching up the strands of the broken necklace, this vision faded before I had time to demand any where or when. And I saw my friend had gone away, laughing at me, back to the others; and after that he was no more my friend in the fairy way. He had seen something in my face which he did not care for. And I let fall the necklace again, but this time I did not stoop to seek for it in the grass that was only fairy grass.

And another time with yet another friend of mine, looking up into his face, a flock of crested birds lighted on a green branch behind him: for he was a master of birds and had called them out of the magic meadows for my delight. But the weight of the singing birds swept the bough down, and for a moment I saw through the leaves and past the bright eyes and hair of my friend, and there was no sky. I saw merely a background without colour or texture, a lid of nothing over the tree, the lovely birds, and the delight I had in my friend. And all at once my mind was flooded with the open blue seen above ploughlands or best in a long narrow street somewhere without birds or delight, when the sky alone and certainly was beauty. And maybe that sky reflected itself into my face, for my friend suddenly dropped his arms from my neck and stepped back from me, his birds darting angrily all round him, and was gone. But for a time that did not matter to me, for I was still picturing the sky above that mean unbroken line of house tops, and I could smell summer garbage—although I did not know it was that, only that my nostrils and stomach were assailed by a sour foulness—and I could hear the wailing of an over-hot baby in a tiny room below the sunbeaten roofs. But I did not know where it was, and after a time the picture died out, leaving me only with a feeling of torsion and darkness at the base of my brain, made no better by my loneliness for my friend who did not come back. There was no place or thing in Fairy Land to which that picture I had seen would fit, and I said to myself that it was nothing which existed. I ate more freely of the joy-apples and lay down more often by the springs and caverns of dreams. But yet I was uneasy, and in the midst of the singing my voice would waver and my pleasure go suddenly blank.

There is yet another thing about Fairy Land which is not well known on Middle Earth. We there have no looking-glasses. Looking was an action which we were used to practise upon others but never upon ourselves. Never were we accosted by this dumb and backless stranger whom Middle Earth women regard as themselves. Never need we fear the hand or face peering around the double's shoulder or smoothing her opposite hair. Never need we perceive change. We lived inside ourselves, seeing only our solid, friendly hands and the front of our bodies from the breasts down. Thus, if our friends told us that we were beautiful, we believed that this was the truth, and it built up in our protected inner selves an assurance which there was no looking-glass to drive out. And yet from time to time it happened to Fairy women that they should gaze too intently into the eyes of their friends and see their own faces, tiny and troubled. Yet if this came to them they would look aside quickly, pretending that nothing had occurred to mar delight, and in a little time, after blossom and dancing and forest chasing, it would be so. Remembrance of the unfit looking would close tight as a poppy bud, and all was well again.

But the time came when I myself was that kind of looker, but, instead of the hasty glance aside and the laugh which is the crying of the inner self for help to the friend, I stayed steady at my looking, and it became plain to me that I was not the same as the rest of the Fairy women. As yet I did not know where exactly the difference lay, nor could I determine whether or not to take some means to allay it. But I went away from my friend, and for a time I was far from the fairy doings and festivals.

During this time of withdrawal I began to suspect, first, that, since I was in some way different from the fairies, I must somehow belong to some other place. Yet I could not anyway imagine what other place there could be, since at that time I had seen no bounds to Fairy Land, and I could not bring myself to speak or question about any subject so alien to all belief. So far this was anything but clear in my mind, yet I discovered myself to be acting, with more and more frequency, in ways that were strange to me if I regarded them critically, but which had some kind of dreadful familiarity which I could not understand.

Thus I would become suddenly anxious as to where and how I should eat my next meal. Although there was fairy food spread ready in any hall, and summer fruits for the thornless plucking. Or it would creep into my thoughts in the middle of a happy game that this was somehow not the thing which I should be doing. Although there was nothing more urgent or more delightful to do in all Fairy Land. Or it would come on me that I must at once and in desperate need wash something dreadful and repugnant from my hands and lips. Although there was nothing to stain them but the pleasant dye of berries or lily pollen. Or I would find myself intently and painfully watching some frond or petal. Although I had never once seen in the fairy glades any shrivelling or withering, or any change that was not willed by the fairy gazers.

And now it seemed to me that the rest of the Fairy folk were becoming ill at ease with me, either avoiding me or else, and oftener, pressing round me too closely. At first I was troubled and constantly seeking to be as I had been, as it seemed to me at first I had always been. Yet the conviction of complete and everlasting companionship was beginning now to waver. With what pain to me! I began to be aware of a dark basis to all my fairy life and delight, of a profound disquiet out of which I had at some time arisen, but which was now again arising round me. I might well shake out the wings of my spirit and dart up from it, yet sooner or later it would be on me again. By and bye the moment came when I must needs face it, not entirely with fear, but with a certain relief. I collected up all the moments of strangeness and memory, trying to make out of them all one coherent image. Then more appeared, which I had to place as best I could. And soon enough I knew, as surely as once I had known the contrary, that there was some place, some existence, other than Fairy Land, and it was from these that I had come.

Now when I knew this, everything became changed. The very colour of flower or vine-leaf quivered under my vision, as though afraid of me, and the faces of my companions too, quivered and became without friendship for me. Thus, I went away through halls and glades, and the magic meadows of shadow runnings where often I had delighted, head-under amongst my own imagined creatures and shapes. Whenever I saw one of the Fairy folk, I would wave a hand of greeting and hurry on as though intent on some new pursuit of an enchanted moment. And after a time I came to the Clefted Ground, where it was necessary constantly to shut eyes and leap. Here I was alone. Yet I was not much frightened of the clefts because I was still as sure-footed as a true Fairy. I did not look down into them, nor did I look up much into the pine branches crossed closely above me. There was light enough, for even here the resiny trunks were dotted with our gay little fairy lanterns, green and orange and pink, fruit-shaped or candle-shaped.

At the far side of a cleft I came on the one we called Serpent coiled round a pine bole and apparently waiting for me. I knew of old that she was not Serpent, but Worm, although it was better not to say so, and I knew suddenly that she was also Traveller-between-Worlds. She was very shiny, and ringed, and blind, with a small shapeless head—but that was of no importance, since her wisdom was not bounded by any constraining skull box, but spread fibrously throughout the length of her body.

"Serpent," I said, "I wish to ask counsel of you."

"Have you a gift?" she said.

"No," said I, "for I had not known until this moment that I would come to you."

"That is as well," she said, "for I do not much care for gifts. They are seldom chosen with sufficient regard for the preference of Serpents. Fairies are not clever in such matters. However, I perceive that you are not a Fairy."

I was silent for a moment then, overcome. The thing had been said, in the remote and toothless voice of Serpent who is Worm. "Are you certain of that, Serpent?" I asked, but my voice did not tremble much. Already I had accepted this, as something at last which would make sense of my pictures.

"As certain as you are yourself," said Serpent; "it is the seventh year, after all."

"The seventh year," I repeated, "and then?" For still I did not know.

"Naturally, they have to pay."

"They. But I?"

"Someone has got to be it."

"What?"

"The teind. The payment." Serpent made a slow gobbling motion, contracting and expanding her rings, which glistened in the pretty light of the fairy lamps. "But there may be others besides you," she added.

"And if not?"

"It has to be paid for. After all, everything has been very pleasant from the point of view of a two-legged creature. For you as well as for them. You need not have looked up nor down. I never look. We elder Serpents have dispensed with such trivialities. You realise, young woman, that only the younger and less knowledgeable Serpents have eyes?"

"Certainly," I said, and curtseyed, for it was no use reminding Serpent that she was Worm. I continued: "But, now that I have looked, I do not think that I care to be the teind."

"You have eaten fairy food."

"That is the least I have done. All the same, Serpent, I propose to find the way out."

"To what place?"

"Wherever it was I came from. Where is that?"

"I am afraid you will have to discover that for yourself. It is likely to be less comfortable than Fairy Land. In any case, you must cross the Debateable Land first."

"How do I get to the Debateable Land, wise Serpent? For I have wandered and wandered in Fairy ground and I cannot find the boundary."

"You could not possibly get out by yourself whatever you found. You will have to meet with a deliverer. And they are scarce. Not always reliable, either. However, if you really intend to leave (and I am becoming drowsy myself) I can give you instructions."

Serpent then explained to me just what I had to do, but the last two or three sentences were trailed out in a softly slimy voice, scarcely audible, as Serpent drooped her worm head down from the pine bole into the cleft, and her rings relaxed in sleep. So I went on my way, following the sinuous edges of a cleft until, as had been foretold, I came to a mound above which the pine branches did not completely meet. One glance up showed me the lidding grey that pressed so terribly close, depthless and formless and utterly sad; I did not continue looking. Knowing that if I considered the matter at too great length I should lose all power of action, I climbed immediately onto the mound and cried out for a deliverer. At once events began to move: the fairy lights on the tree trunks fell into a rapid blinking; one or two even dropped to the ground and flared. A gust of hot air rose out of the cleft beside me and with it a still remote, but very angry, gabbling noise, as though those to whom the Fairies were indebted had become aware that their payment was endangered. A wood bird darted out of the pines, flapped derisive scarlet wings in my face, and sped off, an arrow messenger to screech treachery in some lovely glade. I began to tremble violently. In a moment all would be too late. I could not now even pretend that I had said nothing!

Despairing I looked up just once more, for it seemed to me that the lid too would be shocked into closing down on me. As it was beginning to do. As it was now changing, funnelling down onto me in crushing solid greyness. It was as near as my own choking breath. Their funnel.

And in the funnel there was a hand. It was a large, rather rough hand, with thick nails. It was open and reaching, and I put my own right hand into it. It closed on my hand and I laid my other above, onto its wrist, which I could feel, but not see because of the greyness. And then it lifted me.

Almost immediately everything was swallowed up: the forest, the blinking menacing fairy lights, the wriggling clefts and the mound between them. I could see nothing, hear nothing, expect nothing. I had no measure of minutes or days. I could still feel the hand with both of my own, but there was no ache or drag in the lifting. I was passing through some layer in which such things were altered.

And in the end I found myself standing on a concrete road and grasping in my two hands the crook of a staff, which was warm from my long and firm grip, and made plainly and roughly out of hazel wood.

I had been walking hard for some time and was now resting on my staff and looking back over one shoulder. But there was nothing to be seen so far. I remembered places I had passed. These seemed to be mostly dumping grounds for cast-off things, discarded tins, frying pans, religions, newspapers, dolls, dreams, engines, pulleys, tyres, theories, and so on. It was black night over the road; there were no stars showing, but whether this was owing to their absence from the heaven above the Debateable Land, or because they were hidden by clouds, or, as I then assumed, because they were occluded by the large and powerful arc-lamps at either side of the road, I do not know. This road lay perfectly straight, but dipping and rising a little, for an indefinite mileage behind and ahead of me. Every thirty yards or so there was a lamp standard from whose observation nothing on the road could escape; they were, however, neither friendly nor unfriendly; I was used to them. It was by their light that I had noticed the waste lands on both sides, whose derelict ugliness stretched back from the edges into profound darkness and the beginnings of man's impatience with his destiny.

Here in the Debateable Land there was much that was reminiscent, that brought back to me clear memories, where in Fairy Land I had only perceived faint intimations of something coming increasingly between me and joy. Thus I remembered dumping grounds and back-yards, not so spacious as these, but still devastating enough for the indigenous humans. It seemed to me that I had seen such places very commonly on Middle Earth and that out of that life and place I could remember many more objects which were flawed or broken or chipped or in some way mishandled, than such as were new or tolerably unspoiled. It hurt me now to remember those after the perfections of Fairy Land. It hurt me to think, as I did, of a teapot stencilled crudely with pink and blue, discoloured inside, as I knew well from having washed it so often, and with a crack across the lid. For a time I was overwhelmed with the poverty and inadequacy of that teapot, and of the check table-cloth, hastily darned, as I was now aware, by my mother, upon which I was used to set it every evening. But I pulled myself together, swung my hazel stick, and walked on resolutely.

All things discarded and shed on Middle Earth find their way here sooner or later. As I walked by I could watch the heaps swelling slowly, the hopes and loves effacing one another as the incoming tide effaces a baby's rampart of sand. For a little while the older hopes would be still visible beneath the new ones, then they would be smoothed away and done with. And now I could remember many of the hopes and dreams I had myself cherished in that earlier time, and I could have lain down by the roadside and wept for them, but that I had to hurry on without pause. Only, the memory of what I had wanted for myself and my world as I saw it, made a kind of rough ache in my mind, corresponding to the ache which was now beginning in my feet and ankles, and which I had never known in all the days of my fleet-foot hunting and hour-long dancing in Fairy Land. Thus I remembered kindred pains on Middle Earth, cheap shoes that bit my toes and instep, chilblains, cracked lips, back-ache coming home from the office dog-tired on Spring evenings, my head still full of figures and always at the back the anxiety as to whether one would keep the job, whether the boss had been just snappy or whether he'd meant it, whether perhaps next Saturday—and what would Mother say when I came back, or rather what would we both *do*?

Cogitating upon this it came to me that the thing which I at least had done was, clearly, to go to Fairy Land—or to have been taken there. Yet I could not at present determine any backward limit to my seven years in that country, for right at the beginning it had still appeared as though I had always been there. Or so I thought now.

I looked round constantly over my shoulder, listening intently at the same time, but I could only hear the tinkling and rustling and sighing of the dump-heaps. The road had mounted a slight brow and was now dropping, and I could see that, some distance ahead of me, the lights were reflected in a peculiar way. I was wondering about this when the arc-lamp immediately ahead of me gave a ping and dropped through the centre of its light-cone a flaming question mark which turned to black on the road and shrivelled out, but was enough to sharpen my walk into something near running. Down and down I went as the road dipped and dropped and the lamps dimmed in a rising fog or steam. Then behind me I heard the fairy horns, the long rising scream of the siren, the wild tooting, the speed unchecked on that cornerless road. Looking back from my now breathless running on the bruising concrete, I could see their headlights beginning to lap over the rise in the road, rapidly rising suns. Now I could see ahead of me patches of steam and patches of reflection apparently across the road. Now a plain flood limit lay unescapable but a chance. I could not tell what it was, only it looked dark. Half in, on the edge, lay a piece of machinery with little wheels and a blunt muzzle and a ribbon of cartridges dripping out of its guts. I was in over my shoes as the headlights tipped the crest, but already wreaths of steam were hiding me, rising from the warm blood into the cold night air.

I recognised this for what it was, but where it had been knee-deep in the time of Thomas the Rhymer, it was now almost shoulder-high in the middle, with a slow current that dragged at one's knees and feet. I did not care to swim; I could not face all that blood against my neck and chin. There was no sound now from the horns, no glare from the headlights, the pursuit was checked. Gradually we climbed out of it again, waist-deep, thigh-deep, ankle-deep. In mid-stream I had found a companion. She said: "I was shot while attempting to escape. So I had to wait till someone else came by. Hold me until we are out."

Our clasped hands dripped blood together, strangely from no wounds of our own. I said: "Was it they who shot you?"

"I think so," she said, "but now it is over." I said: "Where can we wash this off us?"

She said: "There is a deep spring near here, of eye-water, tears for the blood. I think that will wash us."

We went down from the road over rocks that were strewn with torn treaties and crumpled telegrams, and washed in the spring. When we came out I found that we were covered with a kind of flexible armour and that it was near dawn. When I asked my companion why, she asked me in turn what else I thought could happen when opposite meets opposite on the same body. And as to the dawn, night had been piling up and piling up in the further side of the Debateable Land which I had just left, and after a time something was bound to alter. I admitted that this was so and asked her for her name. She shook her head and said she didn't know any longer and added that we were now in that part of the Debateable Land where come all that have lived in vain, and this was why we were armoured. We went on together; it was still too dark to see her face at all clearly, and she kept it turned away, partly perhaps because there was a bullet hole in her forehead.

For a time we were walking along the road in silence, very white in our armour of opposites, and then far off I heard the roaring of the sea. As we came nearer I saw a little below the road a bay between black cliffs, and heard the grinding and shrieking of pulled gravel as the great waves pounded and swept forward and back and sideways. And there, fighting the waves with sword and axe and shield were three heroes, each desperate, wearing himself out, each unaware of the others. I asked: "Who are they?" but even as I did so I could see in the dawn light reflecting up from the slithering foam how their faces changed, so that sometimes there was one man and sometimes another. And after a little I observed that one of them was a man whom I had seen more than once on Middle Earth speaking about those things which had seemed to me then to matter more than anything, from a platform in the hall where I was used to go on a Sunday evening when my mother shook her head at me regretfully and went to church; and this man's face now was like his face had been then, and now too his lips were tight and his eyes hard and agonised as he slashed and tore at the leaping water.

And now we were walking through a lovely forest, murmuring in the dawn, where great tree trunks held up uncounted fingers of twig and living leaf. But all at once there was terror in the forest. I saw coming towards us a monstrous flapping thing, white and crumpled, and as it passed it was eating the forest with its formless jaws. "Keep well to the middle of the road," said my companion, and we watched the destruction of the trees by the newspaper and saw the headlines that striped its hideous body dissolve and melt into one another. When it was near us it paused and flapped itself and grinned at us, momently shooting out and withdrawing notebooks, press cameras, fountain pens, cheques and paper laurel wreaths. But we in our armour shook our heads at its antics and walked on quickly. I remembered my boy-cousin who was a reporter on our local paper at eighteen, and how later on his face had changed and gone bright and bitter.

Beyond the forest there was a great concourse of ghosts, old and young, and a great many babies and very young children. They were all round us in the early morning under the now un-lighted lamp standards, and I felt a vile misery creeping through me between my skin and the armour, although I did not believe that the ghosts themselves were unhappy, for they seemed to be talking and playing and doing ordinary things. But I was afraid of seeing my mother among them, or anyone else I had known and loved on Middle Earth, and I stopped on the road with my right hand over my eyes. I still held the hazel stick in my left. It seemed to me now that I could remember the whole of my life on Middle Earth from my shrilly-complaining obscure childhood on to the fright and uncertainty of my adolescence, and the growing dull pressure of working days. And it was all a ghost life. And it was to get back to this that I had left Fairy Land. And as I thought of that I knew also that the pursuit was again near, coming swiftly on me. But I did not care. I was gone soft with misery. I only hoped they might take me back with them so that if only once again I might see and feel the delight I had cast away.

But my companion was crying at me: "Go on! Go on! Very soon I shall be remembering my name!" And she looked up with the oozing bullet hole in her forehead and I thought if I stayed I must recognise her and hear her name, and I was afraid of what it might be, and suddenly I turned away and plunged through the hosts down the road, which narrowed ahead of me to a tunnel. At the end of the tunnel was light, and an immediate chasm. At the far side of the chasm the road began again, apparently the same. At the bottom of the chasm, but not so far down that one could not see clearly, there was an outcrop of extremely jagged rocks and I thought I could also perceive across one of them some pieces of torn cloth and the occasional white of bones. Over the chasm was a rope and plank bridge, just wide enough to walk along, dipping in a curve and without hand-rails. Behind me in the tunnel I could hear the first laughter of the fairies, unpleasantly prolonged by echo, and after all it was impossible for me to surrender to it. My knees were beginning to tremble, but I ran across that bridge, looking steadily at the far side, my head almost bursting with the effort of control, and using my hazel stick for balance. It was very difficult where it sloped up at the far side; I was almost hopeless of being able to make it; when I did reach the road again I lay down flat, shaking, and only just in time unlooped the ropes from the staples and set the chasm between myself and pursuit.

It was now full daylight, although cloudy, and with a rippling wind. The road was very much pleasanter, grass edges and a gravel surface instead of concrete; the lamp standards were gone, and here it wound about through low hills with pasture and woodland and sometimes orchards. There would be farm-houses and barns and byres, and occasionally I saw people working in the fields. Looking through the gate of one barnyard that opened onto the road, I noticed that a chained dragon, elderly, its scales moulting, was being used to blow leisured fire under the boiler of a steam threshing machine, and I saw by the notice attached to the animal's spikes that this was a farmers' co-operative effort.

I was beginning to be hungry and thirsty, so, after crossing a brook, I went down to the edge, knelt on a mossy stone and drank. As I lifted my wet face, the brook said in a grumbling, gabbling voice: "What right have you to drink my water?"

"Please, brook," I said, "I was thirsty."

"All right," said the brook. "But don't make me turn any of your mills."

"Please, brook, I haven't got any mills," I said, and put back the piece of moss which my foot had scraped off the stone. But as I was doing this, suddenly again I heard the sounds of pursuit, the fairies whooping merrily to one another as I had heard it often enough when I was hunter not quarry. I fell on my knees, whispering, my lips against the water:

> "Brook, brook, hide me,
> So the fairies won't find me.
> By power of thirst and hunger and pain,
> So the fairies won't find me again."

I am not sure how that spell came into my head, but I suspect that it had been left lying in the air of the Debateable Land for more years than even the brook could tell. At least it worked, for the brook said: "Very well, my girl, you jump in and be one of my trout."

So in I jumped and was a trout. This was very pleasant and slippery and I saw all kinds of things which I liked, such as bright pebbles and roundnesses, and delicious nosing places under roots, and I blew bubbles out of my mouth and I ate three worms and a wriggling fly cleverly lipped from the dazzling brink of air. But when the fairies came rushing and hulloing over the bridge I was frightened and darted about, though I did not know why, and when one of them threw a pebble down into the brook I darted into the comfort of my deepest nosing place.

And then I was myself again, and I thanked the brook and went on. But I was still hungry and when I saw a bramble covered with big ripe blackberries, I began to eat them. The bramble said, in a scratchy, snarly voice: "What right have you to eat my blackberries?"

"Please, bramble," I said, "I was hungry."

"All right," said the bramble, "but don't cut me back to make any of your tidy hedges."

"Please, bramble, I haven't got a farm," I said, and carefully unhooked the trailer that had caught in my skirt. But as I was doing this, I heard the sound of a second pursuit and knew by the singing that those who came now were the very best of my fairy friends in the old days: the one who had broken the necklace, the one who had been master of birds, and the one into whose eyes I had looked too deep. So I pressed my lips down on the thorns and whispered:

> "Bramble, bramble, hide me,
> So the fairies won't find me.
> By power of thirst and hunger and pain,
> So the fairies won't know me again."

"Very well, my girl," said the bramble, "you jump in and be one of my beetles." So I jumped into the bramble bush and before the thorns had pricked me much I was a very small beetle with six black legs and a double pair of red and purple wings. I was walking up the stem of a bramble because I had started walking up the stem of the bramble, and I went on walking with all my six legs until the fairies rushing and singing by twitched at the

branch and I fell through immense hollows and lights and dark-
nesses, bouncing lightly from stem to stem until I fell flat on my
back on a great leaf. And there I lay, kicking my six legs in the air
because when I was on my back my six legs naturally kicked. In
time one of these legs might have met with a grass-blade onto
which it might have clung, or indeed a puff of wind might have
blown the whole upset beetle right side up. In time any of the
limited number of things which can happen to beetles might
have happened to the beetle I was, but while I was still kicking I
became myself again, lying under a bramble bush wild with rage
and self-pity because my fairy friends had passed me by. In this
frenzy I would have leapt up to run after them, but the bramble
bush had me by the hair, hooked me by the wrist and ankles. By
the time I had loosed myself the frenzy had faded, I thanked the
bramble and went on.

It was, of course, possible that the pursuit might turn and
come racing back on me again, so I went warily through the
pleasant country where Spring and Autumn mingled from one
bend of the road to the next. Yet the look of things was getting
more ordinary; I noticed fewer unicorns and hippogriffs grazing
among the dairy herds or the solid plough-horses; earlier on I
had seen a witch at her cottage door beating a recalcitrant broom-
stick, but now the old ladies I passed were doing nothing more
strenuous than knitting or shelling peas. However, when I saw
someone coming towards me down the road I stepped back behind a wall, gripping my hazel staff, and watched. He was a
middle-aged man in ordinary working clothes, with a cap and
blue woollen muffler knotted round his neck, and thick boots;
his face was heavily lined, especially round the eyes and mouth,

and looked worried, and his hair was going a bit grey, especially where it was clipped short at the back of his neck—though I did not notice that until later. It was clear that he was not one of the fairies, so I stepped out from behind the wall, and he said: "Well, you've been long enough coming!"

"Were you looking for me?" I asked.

"All day," he answered, "and most of this last year as well. Come on now, or we shall be late." And he turned round again in the direction he had been going, plainly expecting me to follow him.

"Are you my deliverer?" I asked, and I think my voice must have shaken a little, for I had been informed by Serpent of the necessary relationship between deliverer and delivered.

"Aye," he said and nodded, grinning at me a little from gapped teeth. "Did you think you'd get a better one?" And he stretched out his hand at me. It was quite clearly the hand I had grasped out of the funnel in the forest, and it was a strong hand; but it was not the questing, beautiful hand of the fairy men, the harp players, the cunning strokers of young leopards. He took my hazel stick out of my hands then, and hit me lightly over the shoulders with it. "Get on!" he said. "We're bound to be out of the Debateable Land by nightfall."

"And then?" I said.

"Why then," said he, "we're man and wife as we're bound to be now the rest of our days on Middle Earth, and what have you to put in to the housekeeping?"

"Well," said I, "if that is so, so it is, and I shall bring my mother's pink and blue teapot and the rest of the crockery, and as many sheets and table-cloths as we're likely to need, the two of us (though it's the truth that most of them are darned here and there), and some bits and pieces of furnishing, the like of a horse-hair sofa (though I have always wanted a good sofa in plush), a flap-table and four cane chairs, an arm-chair that was my Granny's and a hearth rug not much worn. There's upstairs furniture as well—"

"I'll be getting the bed," said he, and put an arm through mine. He was limping a little, and I asked him why. "That's just my leg," he said, "it was plugged by a machine gun at Givenchy. I was thinking the Jerrys had got me that time. I was there bleeding in a shell-hole—ach, hours I was. I can't go running races with you now."

"Never heed," I said, and stroked his arm, "you've got all the blood in you that you need. What's gone's gone. Well then, I've got some kitchen things, saucepans and that, and a good girdle, and I've a nice sewing machine, and what's more, if you lose your job I might still go back to mine, for I used to get four pounds a week in my best time."

"But that was the good years," he said, "you'd never get that now. Not near. But mine's steady. Seems so, anyway, not that there's telling, these days."

We walked along in silence then for a little time, I fitting in my step to his slower one. And I remembered fitting my steps once before to a man's whose arm was round mine. Whit Sunday it was, and a clear day, and we'd walked out miles beyond the bus stop, and he wore a pink tie, the colour of pink hawthorn almost, at least I thought so, and he was a checker at the warehouse up behind my office, and we were going to get a ring and all and he was saving up. And that was seven years ago, before Fairy Land. And I'd been in love with him like the girls in the pictures, and

Mother'd have hot supper ready for us, with scones and jam and a good pot of tea, against the time we got back, for a girl can only be young once. And that was seven years ago.

My deliverer looked round, a bit awkward, and began speaking and stopped, and then said: "One thing. I do like a quiet evening. Not gadding off. You know. Once a week, well, that's all right, but there's a fine lot of books I've got. More than a hundred books, and serious. Would you ever be doing any serious reading, now?"

"That's all right," I said. "I used to be well up in the old days. Evening classes: economics and all that. Though maybe I've dropped out of it lately. But I could pick up."

"Well, there's a bit of luck for me," he said, "you mightn't have been that sort at all for all I knew. But now I look at you, lass, why, I wouldn't wonder if we mightn't go to a meeting now and again, you and me?"

"I used to do all that," I said, "and I did my bit of regular canvassing Election times."

He stopped and took me by the shoulders and said: "We're in luck, the two of us. Why, lass, I mightn't have been that kind of a man at all, and you might have been just any bit of skirt. Not my sort. But you're the kind—" He seemed to be seeking for words, frowning over them, but I didn't know at all what he wanted to say, so I could not help him. At last he went on: "What I was meaning to say was, you're the kind of a lass who might get herself shot. I can see you shot," he said, "with a bullet fair through your head!" And he began to tremble, holding onto me. So I put my arms round his neck and stood close, kissing him. His skin was rough and weathered, sagging a little over the jaw; the grey stubble pricked my cheeks; he smelt of tobacco and machine oil and his own smell. In time he stopped trembling and kissed me harder than I much liked, and said: "That's shell-shock, that was! Never you heed, it comes on all of a sudden and then it's gone. You'll need to get used to it. But I'll be fair right with you."

Evening was now closing down on us, and before us there was a little wood of larches and hazel, with the late primroses between, oh as simple and pretty as could be, and here and there mosses and sometimes fern fronds, lady fern and broad buckler fern, and the bare earth showing, old leaves and good loam. "It was hereabouts I came to cut my stick," said my deliverer. "Sundays we'll come. It's bonnier than the pictures and not so wasteful." He took my hand again and I was not unwilling to feel his strong fingers pressing on mine.

And then out of the wood with a swirl and a crying and a shining of eyes swept the returning pursuit of the Fairies, and in a moment they were all round and clutching at me. I had so utterly forgotten them that I screamed out and caught hold of my deliverer with my other hand and buried my face in his coat.

"Come back! Come back!" they sang quiveringly, softly, and the evening was full of them, tender with memories of delight and magic. Their hands caressed my hair and the nape of my neck, but I burrowed further into the coat between the flannel shirt which I knew well I would be washing next Monday and the inner coat-pocket with the pipe and matches and insurance cards. And I heard deep under the calling of the fairy people the steady mortal heart of my deliverer, the heart strained by war and work but still strong for enough years to see my children growing up and maybe a better world for them.

I lifted my head, and his head too was lifted and white in the evening light, and tough against danger. And the Fairies were gone. We walked through the wood very quietly and down the winding path between the ferns and out over the brae-side, a right bonny path, I thought, and we would go there often, Sundays and Bank Holidays. Lower down, near to the first houses, was the place where the three roads joined, though there was no choice, going this way, of which one we should take. And so we were out of the Debateable Land; and to-morrow would be a working day.

FURTHER READING

For readers interested in discovering more about Naomi Mitchison's oeuvre, here are some references to critical writings not cited in my Introduction.

Bignami, Marialuisa, Francesca Orestano, and Alessandro Vescovi, eds., *History and Narration: Looking Back from the Twentieth Century* (Newcastle: Cambridge Scholars, 2011).

Hubble, Nick, "Naomi Mitchison: Fantasy and Intermodern Utopia," in Alice Reeve-Tucker and Nathan Waddell, *Utopianism, Modernism, and Literature in the Twentieth Century* (Basingstoke: Palgrave Macmillan, 2013), 74–92.

Lassner, Phyllis, *British Women Writers of World War II: Battlegrounds of Their Own* (New York: St. Martin's Press, 1998).

Mackay, Marina, and Lindsey Stonebridge, eds., *British Fiction after Modernism* (Basingstoke: Palgrave Macmillan, 2007).

Montefiore, Janet, *Men and Women Writers of the 1930s: The Dangerous Flood of History* (London: Routledge, 1996).

Murray, Isobel, ed., *The Naomi Mitchison Library Series* (Kilkerran, Scotland: Kennedy & Boyd, 2009–). Murray is the leading scholar on the works of Mitchison.

Oppizzi, Alessia, "Between Gender and Fictional Experiment: Naomi Mitchison's Historical Novels," in Bignami, Orestano, and Alessandro Vescovi, *History and Narration*, 56–84.

Plain, Gill, *Women's Fiction of the Second World War: Gender, Power, Resistance* (Edinburgh: Edinburgh University Press, 1996).

3m

Rec'd

6/2015 **DATE DUE**

			PRINTED IN U.S.A.